# A Special Love
## Just A Little Crush

## Elouise East

# Contents

# 1

# Heath

The car rumbled to a stop in the small parking area, and Heath heard the dogs barking through the closed windows. The moment he opened the car door, the sound of eager and excited animals assaulted his ears. Heath smiled. He loved animals, dogs being his favourite, and had all his life. Becoming a vet was a realised lifelong dream, and there was no place he'd rather be.

Having no idea what to expect when he entered the shelter, Heath grabbed his entire vet bag and traipsed to the reception area. The minute he walked through the doors, several small dogs bounded up to the barrier. Heath nodded at the clever idea of using a gate to stop the dogs from escaping the minute someone entered or exited.

"Can I help you? Oh, you must be Mr Williams! Come on through. Just lift the latch on this side and try to get through the minefield of pattering paws." The humour-filled voice had a very slight Scottish accent if Heath wasn't mistaken.

Heath glanced up and saw a slim man in a purple polo shirt with the shelter logo and a black ball cap shadowing his features, although he could see a dark beard and moustache.

After unlatching and pressing through the gate while holding back the horde, Heath locked it back up and stepped forward to greet the guy. As he reached out his hand, Heath finally studied the man before him—a quick check of his name tag confirmed this was the manager, Rory.

Slightly smaller than he was, Rory was slim but not as slim as he'd first appeared. He had defined shoulder and arm muscles, no doubt needed for this job, with full sleeves of tattoos on each arm. A full black beard covering his lower cheeks and surrounding his narrow lips concealed his face shape. Rory's hair, though hidden in the cap, showed black hair along the sides, so Heath assumed it was short. It was his eyes that caught him, though. Those coffee brown orbs sparkled with humour.

"Nice to meet you, Mr Williams. I'm Rory Stephenson. We spoke on the phone. Spencer is right this way." Rory shook his hand, indicating behind him with a jerk of his head.

"Heath, please."

Heath followed Rory through the building, trying not to trip over the little train of terriers. He was glad he had Rory to follow because the place was like a maze. There were hallways and different-sized rooms all over the place. Finally, they exited to the outdoor kennel area. The setup impressed him. There was a long brick building in which the kennels were situated. Each kennel had an exit door leading out into a grassy area with several metal dividing fences between the individual kennels. He assumed this meant that each dog had the option to stay inside or go outside whenever they wished.

"This is a nice setup you have here, Mr Stephenson. I haven't had the pleasure of visiting the shelter before this. How long have you been here?" Heath concentrated on where he stepped instead of examining the man now walking beside him.

"I've been here for about two months. I'm really enjoying it."

"Where were you before? If I'm not being too nosey by asking," Heath chuckled. "Sorry, it's a fault of mine."

"Nah, it's only a fault if people don't want to answer and you keep prodding," Rory snickered. "I lived with my parents in Perth. I needed a change of scenery."

"Wow, that's a long way to go for a different landscape."

"And that's a story for another day." Rory's eyes twinkled. He smirked and stopped at a kennel door. "This is Spencer. Carlton is with him at the moment; we didn't want to leave him alone until we knew what the prognosis was."

"That's a good call. What did you notice when you first found him?" Heath asked as he entered the brightly lit room and saw a muscular guy sitting on the floor, legs outstretched, stroking the fawn-coloured coat of a gorgeous pug. Spencer's little coal-coloured face was resting on his front paws, but Heath could see his laboured breathing. He indicated for Carlton to remain where he was while Heath knelt on the floor next to the dog; if Spencer was comfortable with Carlton, he didn't want anything to make Spencer more stressed than he probably already was.

"Hey there, Spencer. How are you feeling, little buddy?" Heath ran one hand gently over his fur, feeling the harshness of every exhale and how Spencer's rib protruded. Other than that, he didn't feel overly warm or cold, and his nose was wet and cool, though that wasn't always a sign something was wrong.

Reaching for his bag, he opened the clasp and checked Spencer over as thoroughly as he could in the space he had.

"Okay. Have you noticed any differences in his behaviour or mobility?" Heath asked, packing away his equipment.

"Nothing in his behaviour. He's still a calming influence on a lot of dogs—and people—although, thinking about it now, he has become a little slower in his movements, sometimes dragging his back legs and occasionally needing an extra push to get up any steps. I had put that down to him getting older and having short legs."

"Is he eating and drinking the same as usual?"

Rory nodded. "Yeah. Carlton? You've not noticed him eating any different, have you?"

"No, mate. Nothing changed with that. Just today, I came in, and he didn't greet me at the door like he usually does." Carlton's deep Australian accent had Heath biting his lip to withhold a smile. He loved all kinds of accents, but Scottish and Australian were his favourite. Who would've thought he'd find both in the space of an hour right in Cambridge?

Heath made a note on his phone to avoid showing his smile. "If possible, I'd like to get some tests done on Spencer. From what I see, he seems to be tired, but what you mentioned about his movements can point in other directions. It could just be that he's getting older. But I won't know for definite until I test him."

"Yeah, sure, whatever you think is best."

"How do you usually transport the dogs to the vet?" Heath asked. He was happy to take Spencer with him and get him set up at the clinic now, but he didn't want to mess with their routine if they did it some other way.

Rory rubbed the back of his neck, his cheeks blooming with colour. "Well, usually, Donald Knight takes care of our vet needs, but...um...I had a bit of a run-in with him. Hence the reason I called you." Rory's eyes widened. "Not that I think you're second best or anything. It was just that he was the vet who the previous manager dealt with."

Heath chuckled and waved him off. "I know of Donald, and don't worry, I'm not offended. If you're happy for me to do it, I can take Spencer with me now and get him settled, then as soon as I have a free appointment, I will get the samples I need from him."

"Are you sure? I don't want you to go out of your way."

"I'm heading into the clinic now, so I may as well save you a job later. And it will free up Carlton for some other jobs here, rather than looking after this little champ." Heath scratched Spencer's head.

"If you're sure, then that would be great. We're short-staffed today, so I could definitely use Carlton's help." Rory tucked his hands into his jeans pockets.

"Not a problem. Carlton, would you be able to get Spencer to my car, please?"

"'Course, I can." He rose to a crouch, then scooped Spencer up into his arms.

Heath stood, picked up his bag and stepped towards the door. Rory opened it, holding it for Heath and Carlton before exiting after them. None of them spoke until they got Spencer situated in the cage Heath had in the boot of his car for just these types of situations.

"Right, boss. I'll get started on the next job," Carlton said, walking back towards the shelter.

"Thanks, Carlton. I'll be there in a few."

Rory faced Heath. "Thank you so much for dropping by on such short notice. I appreciate it."

"It's not a problem at all. Even if I am the second choice." Heath fought a grin when Rory's eyes widened again.

"You're not..." He stopped, shook his head and pursed his lips. Wagging a finger at Heath, Rory said, "That's not nice, Mr Williams."

Heath snickered. "Sorry. Couldn't resist."

Rory pivoted towards the shelter, glancing over his shoulder. "Well, you know what they say about second best."

Heath called after him, "What's that?"

"There's always room for improvement!" Rory grinned and waved before entering the building.

Heath laughed, shaking his head. It looked like he and Rory had the same sense of humour.

"Come on, Spencer. Let's get you checked out."

## 2

# Rory

They had been crazy busy for most of the morning and early afternoon when two of their staff had reported in sick. Rory usually kept the shelter at five staff and him, so there were always enough people to cover in case of emergencies. With less staff, it had meant Rory had to postpone his paperwork until then. The paperwork needed for this shelter was the bane of his life. If he'd known the amount he had to do, he might have second-guessed accepting the job.

Probably not, though.

"He seemed like he knew what he was talking about. It would be good to bring someone on that we can go straight to instead of having to ring around for whoever is available. And he's local," Rory agreed.

"He's also not bad to look at." Carlton's eyebrows waggled.

Rory snorted. "Yeah, all right. Keep your libido in check, Australia. I don't want this one to run off." He gave him a mock frown and shooed him away. "Haven't you got work to do?"

Carlton's booming laugh trailed behind even after he left the room, and Rory chuckled. He was right, though. It would not be difficult to have someone who looked like Heath around occasionally. His close-cropped auburn hair showed off the vast array of freckles on his tanned face and neck. He was large but not overly muscly, just enough to manhandle the animals he looked after. There had been two beaded bracelets wrapped around his wrist, giving him an almost earthy appearance. Rory couldn't explain what he meant by that, but it was a word that seemed to fit Heath.

When he laughed, the crinkles around his eyes showed a life full of humour and joy. Something that was severely lacking in Rory's.

The paperwork would not write itself, so he turned his attention back to the figures. The manager's position had come at the perfect time for him. His sister had just married an asshole, and despite Rory's proof that the guy *was*, in fact, a cheating shit, his sister didn't want to know. So, instead of making life more difficult, especially when they'd moved next door to their parents, Rory did the next best thing and used the excuse of finding the perfect job somewhere else.

He had no qualms with his parents, he just knew they would back Aggie regardless, and he didn't need that in his life. He was enough of a disappointment to them as it was.

When he'd moved to Cambridge this past June, three months ago, he'd realised how similar it was to Perth. Not in location or anything like that, but in the sense of it being a city. The part that was the most different was working on the outskirts of the city instead of in the centre. The shelter had a large acreage, allowing for expansion should it continue to be profitable.

As far as Rory was concerned, even if the shelter wasn't profitable, it was still doing a good job. The owner wouldn't keep it running if it didn't make money, though. That much he knew. Mr Harding did not have the patience for any business that suffered losses for more than one or two consecutive years.

Having Heath on board as the main vet would save them the extra money it cost for emergency callouts. He smiled when his thoughts turned to the handsome vet once more. They seemed to have the same sense of humour. It would be nice to become friends with some people outside of work. He knew it would happen eventually, but other than Carlton, none of the staff wanted to socialise outside the property boundaries.

The phone rang, disrupting his musings.

"Good..." his gaze flicked to the clock on his laptop, "afternoon. All Seasons Animal Shelter. This is Rory. How can I help?"

He dealt with several phone calls throughout the afternoon, heading out to help Carlton, Angie and Toby with the cleaning at the end of the day. Carlton was the only other full-time member of staff. The others all worked either two or three full days or five mornings or afternoons. Getting the rota together every month was another arduous task, especially when staff wanted to change for this or that reason. A job which should take around three hours took closer to six. He knew it was because the staff was testing him to see what he would allow. Last month, he'd put his foot down and said he wouldn't do it anymore, but he still had to be fairly lenient; otherwise, he'd lose his staff completely.

After waving goodbye to Angie and Toby, he worked alongside Carlton to finish the lockdown process. Every evening, they locked each of the kennels so dogs didn't escape, and people didn't get in. There had been reports of that happening in the past, too.

Carlton bid goodnight at the end of his shift, and Rory locked the front entrance door behind him. Yawning, he walked towards the office and debated which of his mundane tasks to tackle first.

The phone rang the moment he sat down, and he groaned, realising he'd forgotten to set the phone to closed. Taking a breath, he answered.

"Hey, it's Heath. Sorry, it's late."

"Hey! No problem. Is everything okay?"

"Yeah, yeah. Everything's fine. Spencer is resting now. I took the samples, and they went off to the lab earlier. I should have any results in a few days, depending on how busy they are. The X-rays showed a little arthritis, but it is not enough to explain his gait or any of his symptoms. I mean, it could if he has a low pain tolerance. But I'll wait to see what the labs say."

"That's great, thanks." He yawned again. "God, I'm so sorry. It's been a busy day."

"If it was anything like mine, I can imagine."

They both laughed, commiserating together.

"Thank you again for looking after Spencer for me. I appreciate it."

"It's really not a problem. Any time you need anything, call me. I'm more than happy to help. Even second-best vets are good at their jobs."

Rory chuckled. "I'm never gonna live that down, am I?"

"Probably not." It was Heath's turn to laugh that time. "I know you didn't mean it. I'm only teasing. Just making you a part of the Cambridge world. At least, my version of it."

Rory grinned. "In that case, I'm happy to be a part of that world." He realised after he said it Heath could construe it as flirting, but it was too late to take it back. So, he ignored it and continued, "What are you still doing working, anyway?"

"I'm not. I've just got home. I realised I'd forgotten to ring you. The only number I had was for the shelter. I was expecting to leave a message. So, I should ask you the same question...why are you still at work?"

"I live here." Silence greeted his answer. "Well, on the property anyway. I was catching up on some paperwork when you rang."

"I didn't realise there was a house on the property."

"It's tucked away at the back of the kennels. A little too close to the dawn chorus but nice enough."

"Aww, don't you like your wake-up call?" Heath snorted.

"Let's just say I'm getting used to it."

They were silent for a moment, then Heath said, "I suppose I best get going and leave you to your work. Don't stay up too late, or your alarm clock might annoy you."

Rory chuckled. "I won't. Thanks again, Heath. I'll speak to you soon, no doubt."

"Definitely."

Rory cancelled the call and replaced the phone on the table after clicking it to answerphone. He wanted no more calls interrupting him, even if this last one had been nice.

Heath seemed to be a genuinely nice man. It would be fantastic if Rory could get to know him better. Heath might introduce him into Cambridge society, so to speak. It didn't hurt that, as Carlton had mentioned earlier, he was good-looking. Rory worked too much, and he knew it, but he also couldn't do much about it until he found his feet. The owner was breathing down his neck all the time, making sure he was doing his job properly, and even though Rory knew he was, it was overwhelming.

Maybe he needed to take a night off soon and find someone to take home for a night to relieve some of his tension. Shame he couldn't mix business with pleasure because unless he was mistaken, Heath batted for his team. He wouldn't mess up the chance of a business relationship with him by taking him to bed, though. No matter how much Rory's imagination took him there.

Smiling, he blew out a breath and tackled the rota. The sooner he got it done, the better.

# 3

# Heath

Heath had also volunteered at the shelter several times when he wasn't working as a vet. It was a pleasant change of pace for him, and he got to spend time with dogs for more than a half-hour appointment. He didn't mean to have a favourite, but he always spent the most time with Spencer. The poor dog had many people come and look at him, but as soon as they found out the issues with his health, they chose a different dog. It didn't help that Spencer was thirteen, which was deemed an older dog. Most people coming to look were after the younger, more spritely ones.

Rubbing his hand down Spencer's back, Heath smiled at the look of contentment on the dog's face while they basked in the sunlight while they sat in Spencer's kennel garden. Heath had worn Spencer out by playing tug of war with his favourite plush rabbit, which was bigger than he was. The rabbit and a red Angry Bird plush were the only ones that interested Spencer. God forbid anyone lose or misplace them.

"I'm going to have to get going, Spencer. As much as I'd love to stick around all afternoon, I have some errands to run." He made no effort to stand, though. "Life sucks, sometimes, doesn't it, Spence? You think you find someone you're interested in, spend time with them and are just shy of falling for them when...bam. They drop a bombshell on you. Doesn't matter that I saw it coming. Still knocked me for six."

Spencer twisted his head around, huffed and laid back down again, resting against Heath's thigh.

"Yeah, that's what I thought, too."

"Won't you burn if you stay in the sun too long?"

Heath pressed a hand against his chest, exhaling in a rush. "Jesus, Rory! Give a man some warning, would you?"

Rory chuckled. "Sorry, I thought Spencer's movements alerted you to the fact I was here."

"No, I thought he was commiserating with me."

There was a pause, and Heath was facing away so he couldn't see Rory's face. But then Rory said, "I'm sorry. About your relationship."

Heath snorted. "Thanks. Stupid of me to fall so fast. I knew better."

"Just because you know better doesn't make it any easier."

Careful of Spencer, Heath shuffled around so he could see Rory, who crouched outside the fencing, putting them at eye level. They locked gazes for a few moments, then the bang of Spencer's kennel door sounded, and Spencer was off. Or rather, he was walking with a slight wobble, slightly dragging one of his feet. Heath had noticed it and the fact he needed extra help to get up any steps and had made a note on Spencer's file. Carlton had made some adjustments to Spencer's steps, making them smaller with more of them, allowing him to get up without needing help.

Heath had a feeling he knew what was wrong, but he needed to try some other things first.

"Come into the office and have a coffee before you need to go. I have some aftersun in case you need it." Rory stood and, with a smile, walked back to the main building.

"Unless you want to be bombarded by barks, I would head out now, Heath," Carlton called from the doorway to Spencer's house.

"Yep, on my way."

Heath stood and brushed off the seat of his trousers, striding towards the exit. His face was feeling a little warm, but he wasn't sure whether it was from the sun or from speaking to Rory. Shaking his head, he said goodbye to Spencer and locked the door behind him. So much for being hung up on Alex. He couldn't have been that invested in their brief relationship if he was already feeling...something for Rory. He didn't know what, but he liked him. That was for sure.

"Knock, knock," he said, leaning against the doorframe of the small office.

"Who's there?" Rory mumbled, scribbling away in a notepad.

Heath chuckled. Not being prepared to begin a joke but rousing his inner comedian, he answered, "De Niro."

"De Niro who?"

"De Niro I am to you, the more I like you."

Rory snorted, dropping his pen to the table and covering his face. Heath chuckled at his response. The joke was kind of crappy and a little flirty, but it didn't bother Heath as much as he thought it would.

"Thanks, Heath. I needed that." Rory wiped his eyes with the bottom of his polo shirt, revealing a smooth area of slightly tanned skin for a too-brief moment.

"Having issues?" he asked, pointing at the paperwork.

Rory shook his head. "Nothing more than usual. I'm sure the paperwork multiplies, though. Maybe I need you to neuter the paperwork instead of the dogs."

Heath laughed, entering the tiny room and pulling out the wooden chair in front of the desk. He could barely see the computer for the piles of paper on it. "Do you even have a filing cabinet?"

Rory thumbed over his shoulder as he nodded. "Yep, underneath that pile of paperwork there."

"You realise the filing cabinet is for putting paper *inside* rather than on top, don't you?" Heath crossed his arms, watching intently when Rory's cheeks coloured.

"I'm well aware, Mr State-the-Obvious. But until I get the time to sort out the mess the previous manager left me with, it has to stay as it is." Rory tilted his head towards the piles of paper. "This is all *their* doing, not mine. I'm trying to get through it all so I can file it away. I just don't have enough hours in the day."

"Can you not hire someone to help you?"

"I don't have the funds. Nor will the owner provide any."

"You can't kill yourself off over the job, Rory. You need to take some time for yourself." Heath leaned forward, resting his elbows on his knees.

Rory's face softened. "I will. Eventually." He smiled. "Ooh, I said I would get you coffee." He went to stand, but Heath waved his back down.

"Nah, I'm good. I need to head out. I've been thinking—"

"That's dangerous coming from you," Rory snarked good-naturedly.

Heath narrowed his eyes. "*I've been thinking*...if you have a picture of Spencer, I could put it at the clinic and mention it to the people who come in. It might not do any good, but I could take some business cards as well and see if I can send more people your way."

Rory gawked at him, then seemed to shake himself. "That would be amazing. I know we have all the dogs listed on our website, but there is nothing better than word of mouth."

"No problem. Also, I don't think Spencer's issue is arthritis. He's been on these injections for a while now, and I haven't seen any improvement. If anything, it seems to be worse. I believe I know what is wrong, but I'd like to get a second opinion first. Is that all right with you?"

Rory's face became pained. "Yeah, of course. I had hoped I was imagining him getting worse, but I was right." He shook his head. "Why does it happen? Why can't everyone live nice, healthy lives?"

"The world would be full of pretentious assholes if that happened. There must be some sort of karma. It's just a shame it happens to the good people and pets, too." Heath had said it to make Rory laugh, but all he got was a small smile. "I'll get the second opinion as soon as I can. See you soon."

"Hey, Heath?" He turned to face Rory, who was standing in the doorway. "What do you think it is?"

He sighed. "I think it's degenerative myelopathy. It's a genetic neuromuscular condition."

"Is it treatable?"

Heath stepped closer. "No. I'm sorry, but no."

Rory closed his eyes and clenched his jaw. "Fuck," he mumbled, then heaved a sigh.

Heath rested a hand on his shoulder and squeezed. "I may be wrong, Rory, but I honestly don't think I am."

"It's okay. It's not your fault. Just...why can't it happen to horrible dogs instead of nice ones."

"Even horrible dogs were friendly once upon a time."

"I know," Rory agreed, pouting, which Heath found rather endearing.

"Will you be all right?"

Rory nodded. "Yeah. I always am." He tried for a smile and failed, so Heath made a note to ring him later and make sure he was. He hated leaving him alone after giving him the bad news.

"I'll head out to help Carlton instead of doing paperwork. It will get my mind off it."

"All right. I'll speak to you soon."

# 4

# Rory

A few days later, Heath had his answer, and so did Rory. Spencer *did* have degenerative myelopathy. Heath explained that there were no tests they could do to confirm the condition, but after removing some of the other potential conditions through tests or trial and error of treatment, it was the only one left.

It had been hard enough to get anyone interested in adopting Spencer because of his age as it was; now, Rory knew it would be next to impossible for the amazingly gentle and cheeky dog to find a home. It wasn't fair.

Because of the unfairness of it all, Rory had splurged a little—from his own pocket, mind—on some advertising for Spencer. Although he couldn't lie about his condition and potential medical costs, he could explain how loving and gentle the dog was. Spencer would be perfect for a less active family, not completely inactive, though, because Spencer loved his walks, even if he was slower and had an uneven gait. If it wasn't for his diagnosis, no one would think there was anything wrong with Spencer just by looking at him.

The news had cast a darker shadow over the shelter for everyone, not just Rory. They all loved Spencer. Even Heath, who always found time to spend with the little pug when he was there. It was a shame one of the staff couldn't adopt him.

"Hey," a quiet voice said.

Rory turned his head to greet them. "Hey, Carlton. Everything okay?"

Carlton nodded. "Yeah, I saw you staring off into space. I wanted to make sure you were all right."

It was Rory's turn to nod. "As right as I'll ever be," he joked weakly. His gaze returned to the kennel building. "You would've thought I would be used to it by now."

"Used to what?"

"Dogs not getting adopted or having to be put to sleep. As much as I despise the idea, I know I have no choice with Spencer unless I can find him a home. The owner won't waste," Rory used finger quotes, "his money on vet bills indefinitely."

"The bills won't be that excessive, will they?"

Rory glanced back at Carlton. "Not huge because there is no treatment for the condition, Heath said, but as his condition worsens, extra vet appointments might be necessary. I don't know, in all honesty, Carlton. We can't predict how it will go."

They were silent for a moment. "Couldn't we raise some money to cover his future costs? That might make things easier on a potential adoption."

Rory considered the idea. It had merit. The person who adopted Spencer would still have to pay the fee to take him home, but maybe the staff could offset some of the medical costs and entice more people to look the dog's way. "It's something to consider. I'll have a think. Ask around the other staff for me, please, and see if they have any ideas we could use."

"Will do."

"Thanks, Carlton."

"You're welcome." He paused, and Rory saw the corners of his mouth turn up. "You could always ask your vet to adopt him."

Rory's eyes widened. "He's not my anything. We're friends."

Carlton raised his eyebrows. "That's not what I see, but whatever. You should still ask him. He spends plenty of time around Spencer, and he has the medical knowledge of how to help him."

"I'm sure Heath has enough on his plate without adding a dog into the mix," he protested.

Clapping him on the shoulder, Carlton smirked. "Ask him anyway." He spun around, and Rory watched when he headed to the storage building.

In an ideal world, Heath would adopt the happy little dog, but Rory was not delusional. This was not an ideal world.

• • • ● • ● • ● • ● • •

Heath's voice drew Rory to the kennels by. The guy was in Spencer's garden again, playing fetch and tug of war with the red Angry Bird plush that Spencer usually carried around the place in his mouth.

"Fetch, boy!" Rory watched while Heath threw it to the opposite side of the pen, then crouched down and cocked his head to the side, rubbing a hand across his jaw. When Spencer returned, Heath gave him a lot of fuss, sitting cross-legged on the grass while Spencer scrambled to climb on him. "Who's a good boy? Yes, you are. How are those legs of yours, Spencer? Still making things difficult, I see. Well, I'll see what I can do to help. Okay, boy?"

Rory's eyes filled with the care and attention this surprising man gave to any animal, but especially Spencer.

"You could adopt him, you know." The words were out before he thought about it and, in the process, made Heath curse.

"Fuck, Rory!" He shook his head. "I need to stop putting my back to the exit," he mumbled, Rory only just hearing.

Smiling, Rory agreed, "Yes, you do if you're that jumpy."

Heath narrowed his gaze, all the while stroking his hand across Spencer's fur. "I'm not jumpy. You're good at creeping up on people."

"Well, it's good to know I would ace being a spy if I ever wanted a change of career." Rory stuck his tongue in his cheek to stop him from laughing.

Heath shook his head, snorting. "Rory's being silly, Spencer. Whatever shall we do with him?"

At his name, Spencer lifted his head to look at Heath, then repositioned his head on Heath's leg, now outstretched. Rory took in the contented demeanours of both man and dog and reaffirmed Carlton's words from earlier that day.

"You could adopt him," Rory repeated the words he'd said in lieu of a greeting.

Heath was quiet. "I've been thinking about it. At the minute, I can't with my workload being as it is. It wouldn't be fair to Spencer. When I hire a new vet to help me cope, if he's still here, I'll definitely consider it."

Rory's heart soared at the potential solution. "Carlton brought up the idea of hosting a fundraiser for Spencer. He said we could raise some money towards future medical costs to help a potential owner.

"That's a great idea." Heath's gaze flicked over Rory's shoulder. "You're needed." Heath nodded towards the main building.

Rory looked over his shoulder to see Edith waving him over. He sighed. "No rest for the wicked, eh?"

"Why rest if you're wicked? Too many fun things to do." Heath grinned when Rory rolled his eyes.

He stood, staring down at Heath with his hands on his hips. "You're not funny, Mr Williams." He pivoted and aimed for Edith, who ducked back into the building when she saw he was coming.

"Yeah, I am," he called after Rory, "You just won't admit it."

Rory couldn't help but smile. Heath was something he hadn't expected to find in Cambridge, but he was glad he had. Although they weren't friends enough to socialise outside of the shelter—yet anyway—Rory felt he could call Heath a friend, nonetheless.

While he dealt with the adoption query Edith had, his mind wandered back to the fundraiser. He'd need to get permission from the owner first, but that shouldn't be too hard if he highlighted the increased chance of finding Spencer a family. The owner had no fondness for any type of animal, so Rory had never understood why the man owned an animal shelter until he realised it was all about money for the guy. Rory couldn't imagine not caring about animals like he had done all his life. Many times, in his younger years, he had been yelled at when his parents had found animals in his room where he was caring for them. There had been a baby bird he had helped to grow, which luckily his parents had only found out about once the bird was old enough to fly away; and a hedgehog he had smuggled into a box under his bed to keep warm when he'd found it in a room downstairs during a snowstorm. There were several more times that they didn't know about, too.

Rory's mouth curled when he thought about those animals. Everyone had thought he would become a vet, but he'd soon found out he was too squeamish for that. Vomit, shit and piss he could deal with. Blood, organs and anything like that, he couldn't. He didn't faint or anything, but it made him heave.

Returning his mind to finding a solution for Spencer, he was determined to find someone suitable. There must be someone besides Heath who would look after such an amazing dog, despite his limitations and age.

He decided to contact the owner right then and see if he could get the ball rolling on the fundraiser. No time like the present.

# 5

# Heath

By the time it came to closing at four—and he'd never been as glad of an early closing day on a Thursday before—he was shattered. Elaine had done an amazing job on reception, and Heath made a note to increase her wage if he could next month or at least give her a bonus.

As it was, he had closed at four forty-five instead because a last-minute appointment had come through. A woman had brought in her children's pet rabbit to be checked over because the poor thing had been shaky and quiet in relation to her normal behaviour. It had taken him too long to explain that the rabbit was pregnant and to assuage her fears.

Finally, though, the door was closed and locked, and Heath could relax. He collapsed into a chair in the waiting room, staring across at Elaine.

"What the hell was that all about?" he asked her.

Elaine leaned her arms on the desk in front of her. "It was two-fold, I think. Some customers said they had appointments with Donald Knight, but his wife took him to hospital with appendicitis."

"Oh, no. Is he going to be all right?"

Elaine nodded. "Yes, I spoke to his wife briefly to ask if there was anything we could do, but she declined."

"At least Donald is where he can get sorted. Bet he's hating it." Heath chuckled.

"I bet."

Heath tilted his head. "And the other reason?"

Grinning, she turned back to the computer. "You have come highly recommended by one Rory Stephenson."

A blush stole into his cheeks, but he tried to hold back his smile. "That's nice of him."

"Uh-huh. I know something is going on between you two. You may as well tell me." Elaine scooted her chair back and stood, pushing it back into place before crossing her arms.

"Nothing is going on between us." Heath stared at the floor, wishing he was lying.

"But you want there to be."

"Okay. Yes, I do. But he's busy all the time, and so am I. What's the point when we can't find the time to be together. It's better to not try anything, then we won't get disappointed."

"So, you're giving up. Just like that. Just because it might be hard work." She frowned. "That's not the Heath I know. There's something else you're not telling me."

Heath hated she was so observant, but she was right. He sighed, shoulders slumping. "I don't need another Alex." Elaine knew everything about Alex. She had been the one to call Heath on his sappy, exuberant behaviour after he'd met Alex for the first time on the double date with Marcus. He'd happily filled her in with all sorts of information over the few weeks they were together. Then, when shit hit the fan, and it all blew up, Elaine also noticed and commiserated.

"Why do you think Rory is the same as Alex? Has he shown some similar behaviour?" She decreased the space between them, folding herself into the chair across from him.

"No, nothing. I guess…"

"You're scared," she said, leaning forward to rest her elbows on her knees.

Heath raked his fingers through his hair, which was longer than he usually had it. It needed cutting. He dropped his hands and exhaled in a rush. "Yes. I'm scared," he admitted.

Elaine sighed. "There is nothing I can say to make that worry go away. I wish there was. But you need to remember that Rory isn't Alex. They are two separate people. You wouldn't like it if someone said you were just like Donald Knight, would you? You're both vets. Surely you're alike?" She quirked an eyebrow.

He could see where she was going with the conversation, but it didn't help him stop the nervous feeling he got every time he considered asking Rory on a date. Heath may put up a confident front, but he was quite shy. No matter what he said, there were similarities between Rory and Alex: they both had the same sense of humour, which was what attracted Heath to them in the first place, and they both had stressful busy jobs. The major difference was that Rory didn't appear to have an unrequited crush on someone else.

"All right. If I see an opening during one of our conversations, I'll try to ask him out. How's that?"

"Perfect."

Rolling his eyes, he stood and headed to his clinic. "Don't leave Jim home alone too much longer; you never know what he'll cook for you!" he called over his shoulder with a laugh.

He entered his office to the sound of his mobile ringing, and he rushed over to grab it. Seeing it was Marcus, he answered with, "Were your ears burning?"

After a slight hesitation, he said, "No. Why?"

"I was just talking to Elaine about you in a roundabout way."

"Good things, I hope." He laughed.

"Always." Heath grabbed his bag, resting the phone between his ear and shoulder while he used both his hands to collect all his things together. "Anyway, what's up?"

"I wondered if you wanted to join me with the guys?"

Heath stood up straight, holding the phone once more but staring out of his office window. "Seriously?" He honestly couldn't believe that Marcus had asked him. It hadn't been that long since Alex had broken up with him. Surely, the guy didn't want him encroaching on his new relationship.

"Sure. They all know you. No one will mind if you're there too." He heard Marcus sigh. "I want my best friend to come out with my other friends, Heath."

"I'm sorry, Marcus, but I can't. Not at the moment. It's still too fresh. Alex wouldn't want me there as a reminder of him seeing someone when he was in love with someone else."

"It's not with th—"

"No, Marcus. Thanks for the invite, but no. Let me know when you're free, though. I think it's my turn to buy the shots, this time."

Each time they went out together, he and Marcus would alternate who bought the first shots of the night. They usually picked three different flavours, then threw them back before deciding on what else they would drink that night, which in Heath's case was usually beer.

"First, I'm not talking about Crush. It's the guys from the gym, all right. I doubt I'll be going back to Crush any time soon. Even if it has been two months since I last spoke to Casey." Marcus sighed. "You never know. You might find someone you'd be interested in."

"Marcus, do not go setting me up on a date!"

"Oh, calm your nipples! I wasn't planning to. I just thought it would be nice for you to meet some new people. Your social circle is tiny. You can't work all the time."

"I know that, and I'm not. I've started helping at the animal shelter."

"Which one? And why? Haven't you got enough vet work to do?" Marcus sounded exasperated, which Heath could understand because he *was* always busy.

"Yes, I do, but I enjoy hanging out with the dogs. You know they are my second favourite animal."

"I know, I know. Hedgehogs are your first." He sighed again.

"You mean well, Marcus. I know you do, but you need to let me do this my way. I'm sure I will come out with your friends, eventually. Just not yet, okay?"

"Sure. Are there any hot guys at the shelter?" Marcus mused.

"Well, as luck would have it, there is a very nice Australian and a rather tasty Scot." Heath smiled, though he knew Marcus couldn't see it.

"Ooh, I know that tone. Which one do you have your eye on?"

Heath hadn't meant to let on that he liked one of them, but Marcus knew him too well. "The Scot. Rory. We've been talking a lot when I've been there helping. He's a nice guy. Busy but nice."

"What more could you ask for? When are you going on a date?"

"I've not asked him yet."

"Heath! Jesus, man. Just ask the guy already."

"I will! I've already had this discussion with Elaine tonight. I don't need more grief from you."

Marcus snorted. "Well, no. If you've received it from Elaine, I'll let you off. But I want to meet him. I feel the need to seek out a dog."

"No, Marcus. Leave me be."

"Nope."

And the bastard hung up.

# 6

# Rory

"Have you seen Beethoven? And the ones after it?" Rory asked while he tried to keep a golden retriever still so Heath could work on its cut paw. The poor thing had stepped on something on their walk that morning, and Rory had immediately taken him to the clinic. Nothing to do with being able to see Heath again or anything, naturally.

Heath gave him a droll look, then refocused on Baxter. "Who hasn't seen them? I prefer Turner and Hooch, though."

"Yeah, that was good. I don't think there are many dog films I haven't seen. Even the animated ones."

"A movie buff, are you?" Heath said as he cleaned the wound, making the dog flinch and whine before covering it with a bandage.

"Definitely. It's what I do when I don't work." Rory paused. "Which isn't very often, I admit." He laughed.

"In which case, would you like to go to the cinema with me?"

Rory gazed at Heath while he finished working, wishing the guy would look at him so he could get an idea of whether it was a date or just a night out with a friend. When the silence stretched out, he answered, "Yeah, that would be great. Do you know what's on at the minute?" He was glad his voice sounded semi-normal.

"To be honest, I don't have a clue. Let me wash up, then I can check my phone."

Rory studied the man's actions while he cuddled with Baxter, allowing the dog to lick his face as Rory scratched behind his ears.

"All righty, then."

Heath pulled his phone from his pocket and rested back against the counter across from Rory. With Heath focusing on his phone, it gave Rory time to examine his features. The usually closely cropped hair had grown out some since he first met Heath back in September, and it was a style that looked good on him. Anything would suit him. Heath's freckles, while still there, were less visible now that the sun had stopped darkening them.

"Here are the choices." Heath came to stand next to him and tilted the screen so Rory could see. "It all depends on when you'd like to go, I suppose?" Heath reached up to scratch his jaw, their shoulders brushing.

Rory tried to concentrate on the screen, but it was difficult. "Um...why don't you choose? I'm happy to watch pretty much anything."

"Okay, as you seem to trust me so much, I'm going to surprise you." Heath smirked. "What about after work on Friday?"

Rory's gaze roamed over Heath's face, seeing his eyes crinkling with mirth. "Fine by me."

"Great. I'll swing by to pick you up about six-thirty."

"No, don't come out of your way. I'll meet you there."

Rory saw Heath's eyes tighten, but he grinned and nodded. "Okay."

There was a knock at the door, and Elaine popped her head in. Rory had come to know her through their phone conversations, but it had been nice to finally put a face to a name.

"Mr Holland is here with Beatrice."

"Thanks, Elaine. We've just finished."

Elaine's eyes flicked from Rory to Heath, and a small smile played on her lips. "I'm sure."

She closed the door behind her, and Rory frowned at Heath. "What was that about?"

Heath glanced away and walked around to the other side of the table. "No idea."

Rory raised his eyebrows but left it alone. "Right. I better get going then. Come on, Baxter. Let's see if Carlton has burned the place down yet."

They both laughed, and Rory exited the treatment room. He stopped by reception to sign the paperwork and pay for the appointment, but Elaine waved him off.

"Heath said he'd sort your bill later."

Rory nodded and bid goodbye, carrying Baxter to the car. Unable to believe he was going out with Heath in three days, he smiled the entire journey back to the shelter.

"Wow, what's *that* smile for?" Emma said as he walked in the door.

"What smile?" Rory tried to dial back his grin but found he couldn't.

Emma chuckled. "*That* smile." She pointed at his face. "The cat has got the cream smile. Who made you so happy?"

"That would be the vet, I bet," Carlton stated, walking into the foyer.

"Well, aren't you a poet," Rory shot back, heading for the back.

Unfortunately, they both followed when he carried Baxter to his kennel and settled him in with some fresh water and a treat.

"Did he ask you out? Did you ask him out? Did you make out?" Emma babbled, keeping up with him when he strode towards the building once more.

"Emma! Please!" Rory stopped, Emma crashing into the back of him. "Fine." He faced them with his hands on his hips. "Heath asked me to go to the cinema with him on Friday night."

"Yeah!" Emma and Carlton fist bumped.

"It's not a date."

They both frowned at him. "But you just said—" Carlton started.

"I know. But I don't think it's a date. I think we're just going as friends." Rory could hear the uncertainty in his own tone.

Carlton stepped forward. "It would surprise me if this wasn't a date, Rory."

"How do I know?" Carlton and Emma shared a look, which Rory decoded to mean they had no idea. "Don't worry about it. I'll just see how it goes." He drifted off with a wave and went to his office. Paperwork was calling. He wasn't hiding at all.

• • • ● ● • ● ● • • •

When Friday arrived, Carlton told Rory to leave early and he would lock the place up. Rory had argued, and they'd eventually agreed that Carlton would lock up most things, but Rory would lock up behind Carlton before he headed out.

After he showered, Rory stood in front of his wardrobe and flicked through his clothes. He didn't know what to wear. The cinema was air-conditioned, that much he knew, so he didn't want anything that would make him too hot, but the night air, being the end of November and all, was on the chilly side.

Finally, he decided on a burgundy, v-neck jumper, which his mother had brought him a couple of years ago, and his worn dark-wash jeans. Feeling as comfortable as he was going to get, he checked the time and left early instead of standing and pacing a hole in the carpet. The car took a mile or so to warm up, but then it was blasting heat at him. He'd been spot on with the outdoor temperature.

Parking in the cinema car park, he kept the engine running to keep him warm and pulled out his phone. He still had around forty minutes until he was supposed to meet with Heath, so he checked his social media, updating a couple of things on the shelter's accounts, too.

A knock by his ear made him screech and drop his phone. Rory squinted through the window to see Heath standing there, smiling. Exhaling heavily, Rory turned off the engine and stepped out, quickly slipping into his coat and buttoning it before rooting around in the footwell for his phone.

"Hey," Rory said when he had settled enough to face Heath. "Sorry about all..." He waved his hand towards his car as if that explained everything about his behaviour.

"No problem. I didn't mean to make you jump."

"It's fine." Rory burrowed inside his coat, glad he'd brought the thick woollen coat he had used regularly in Scotland.

"Are you ready?"

Rory nodded. They walked in silence for a few steps until Heath broke it.

"How's Baxter?"

Rory appreciated the subject, thinking it would allow him to figure out where this whole...cinema thing was going. "He's doing fine. He can put weight on it again now, but he's still running with a slight limp."

"Yeah. It's probably still feeling a little bruised. He'll be back to normal in no time."

They entered the cinema, Heath holding the door open for Rory to go through first.

"I've already bought the tickets. I just need to collect them."

"Are you going to tell me what we're watching yet?"

Heath grinned, showing his teeth before replying, "Nope."

Rory huffed and shook his head. He had no idea what he'd let himself in for.

Turning his body so Rory couldn't see the screen, Heath laughed at Rory's curse while he printed off the tickets, tucking them straight into his pocket where Rory couldn't reach. They queued up behind some teenagers and waited to get some food and drink.

"Now, are you a popcorn or sweetie cinema-goer?" Heath side-eyed him. "Because this might be the end of our friendship, depending on your answer."

Rory rolled his lips in to stop himself from smiling. When he knew he wouldn't embarrass himself, he replied, "There is only one answer that is good enough. Both."

Heath sighed over-dramatically and wiped pretend sweat from his forehead. "Thank god! You worried me there for a minute."

They ordered a tub of popcorn to share, and a bag of sweets and a drink each. Heath paid, refusing Rory's money. "I asked you here, so I pay."

Rory huffed and followed Heath towards the double doors, heading for the cinema screens. He tried to peek at the film title as Heath handed over their tickets, but it was too small for him to see. Heath smirked at him and led the way. Rory didn't care if Heath was leading him to the edge of a volcano. He was beginning to believe he'd follow Heath anywhere.

Sitting beside Heath in a darkened cinema, along with the scent of popcorn and sweets, took Rory back to his teenage years when he'd take dates and make out in the back row. It had only happened once or twice, but the reminder set his pulse racing. Wiping his palms on his jeans, he fidgeted before reaching for a handful of popcorn. His heart rate increased more when their fingers brushed against each other.

Rory had been over the moon when the film had started. It was a special showing of A Dog's Journey, and he couldn't believe Heath had found a dog film to watch, especially after their conversation earlier that week about loving films about dogs.

They didn't do much talking through the film, but they had caught each other's gaze occasionally, and Rory could feel something arc between them. When the film finished, they gathered their rubbish and trailed into the chilly night, zipping up their coats.

Before Rory could push his hands into his pockets, Heath slid his hand into Rory's, threading their fingers together. Heath peered at him, a small smile on his face, and Rory's heart skipped a beat.

"Are you up for a short walk?" Heath asked after clearing his throat.

"Sure."

Heath led him along the road and around a corner, where he gasped.

"Oh, my god!" Rory stopped, and from the corner of his eye, saw Heath studying his face. Rory couldn't stop his mouth from opening and closing while his attention roamed around the area in front of him as if he didn't know where to look.

When Rory shivered, Heath pulled him close, tucking their joined hands in his oversized pocket to warm them, and started wandering down the street. Each house had lights decorating the outside walls in various designs, which highlighted everything around him in an ethereal glow, and in the gardens stood numerous displays—Santa, reindeer, sleighs, bells, everything you can imagine. It was truly a winter wonderland.

"This is amazing! How did you know this was here?" Rory asked.

"A friend told me about it. I saw it for the first time last year." Heath explained about the large display of Christmas lights, but not just any lights. The houses on this street had a competition every year to see who had the best display. The idea behind it was that when you had seen them all, you were to choose your favourite and drop some money into the box at the end of the driveway. All proceeds, regardless of who won, were donated to a charity. Heath told Rory that he believed they had made over three thousand pounds the previous year.

"That is a fantastic idea. Maybe we could do a similar thing at the shelter to raise some money." Rory cocked his head. "Hmm. That will need a bit of thought before I decide anything. I'm not sure if the lights will bother some of the dogs."

Rory caught Heath watching his reaction several times, and he never complained about the—very—slow pace, so Rory could inspect every item in every garden. When the night air became a little too cold, Heath pulled Rory closer.

They came to a stop halfway down the street, Heath wrapping his arms around Rory's waist and gazing at him. "I really like you, Rory," he whispered, his words leaving on a cloud of air.

Rory slid his hands up Heath's coat and linked them behind his neck. "I really like you, too."

Heath smiled, lowering his head slowly as if to allow Rory time to change his mind, and skimmed his lips across Rory's mouth before pressing closer. Heath ran his tongue along the crease of Rory's closed lips until he gasped and gave Heath entry. Moving one hand from Rory's waist to cup his jaw instead, Heath deepened the kiss. Rory explored the warmth of Heath's mouth. They tangled their tongues, breath coming faster until they had to break for air.

Steam billowed around them from the heaviness of their breathing, but their gazes never left the other's face.

"Wow," Rory mumbled, a dazed feeling surrounding him.

"Yeah." Heath cleared his throat. "Let's head back to the cars. I don't want you getting too cold."

They strolled back down the street, Rory's arm linked through his own and his head on Heath's shoulder, only stopping once for Rory to drop some money into one of the gardens.

# 7

# Heath

He'd not been able to get to the shelter that week because of the influx of patients he was still receiving after Donald's absence. Although the man was on the mend, thankfully, he wouldn't be returning to his job for a few weeks, so Heath had continued to accept clients in his absence. He didn't mind, to be honest. After all, he became a vet because he wanted to help animals, and that was what he was doing.

Heading home after another long day, Heath tried to contain his excitement. Rory had called that afternoon, inviting him for dinner, so Heath had to hurry to make sure he was ready by the time Rory arrived, which only gave him an hour. A shower was the primary requirement, and then clothes. Apart from that, everything else would be if he had time.

Cursing up a storm when he stubbed his toe on the corner of the bed, Heath towel-dried his hair with one hand and opened a drawer with the other, pulling out grey trousers. Throwing the towel in the vicinity of the washing basket, Heath grabbed some briefs and hobbled over to the wardrobe, his toe still pounding with pain. Matching the shirt to the trousers would be no use because he didn't own any grey shirts, so white would have to do. He dismissed the idea of a tie because he didn't want to be too formal. He'd asked Rory what the dress code was—he had no idea where they were going—and Rory had replied that it was smart but not meeting the Royal family smart. Heath chuckled, remembering that description.

After dressing, he checked his watch, seeing he had ten minutes to spare. He didn't need to do anything with his hair, thankfully—a close-crop style made things much easier for him—but he splashed on some cologne. Then, although they would disappear beneath his shirt sleeves, Heath slid on his bracelets. He rarely left them off, especially because they had been a gift from his brother; it meant a lot to him.

When the doorbell rang, he was ready and waiting and flung the door open quickly, to Rory's surprise.

"Are you excited by any chance?" Rory's mouth quirked up at the corner.

Heath felt the heat suffuse his cheeks, unable to look away from Rory. "Yes." Croaking his reply, Heath focused on the man in front of him. Rory was wearing black trousers that must have been tailor-made for his body, an emerald green shirt and a black, unbuttoned waistcoat underneath his thick coat. Alongside his black beard and hair, it made him look like a movie star. He was gorgeous.

"Heath?" Rory's amused voice broke Heath from devouring him with his eyes.

"Sorry." Heath shook his head slightly, trying to clear his muddled brain. "What did you say?"

Rory pursed his lips as if trying to stop himself from laughing. "Are you ready to go?"

"Yes!" Heath winced when his words came out at a shout, and he reached for his coat. Ignoring Rory's chuckles, he flicked off the hallway light and closed the door behind him. "Are you going to tell me where we're going yet?"

Rory shook his head. "No."

When they settled in Rory's car, Heath asked something he'd been wondering about for a while. "How come you don't use some of the...words that Scottish people say?" Heath scrunched up his face. "I mean, I've heard Scottish people say Scottish words for things, but although you have the accent, you don't have the dialogue, for want of a better word."

Rory was silent for a moment, then sighed. "I taught myself not to, even when I was still in Scotland. I love Scotland and the language, but I wanted to...stand out, I suppose, when I was younger." Rory ran a hand over his beard before continuing, "It stuck with me, and I can't seem to get out of the habit now."

Heath was sure there was an underlying reason for Rory making that decision, but he refused to push. "As long as you are happy with who you are, you don't need to change for anyone."

They said nothing further until Rory parked the car, Heath understanding he'd brought up a subject Rory was less than enthused about. Seeing they were at a Chinese restaurant on the opposite side of the city from where Heath lived, he grinned.

"Is this okay?"

Heath glanced over. "More than okay." Heath had only ever been there once, but he loved the way it was all set up.

The front of the restaurant appeared dark as they approached, but the restaurant had tinted windows, making it look like they were closed when, in fact, they weren't. Rory held the door open for Heath to enter, and Heath inhaled deeply the scents of cooking oil, seasoning and ingredients that made his mouth water. Rory led him to the hostess's podium, and they followed the woman to their table. Dark wooden beams rose throughout the open-plan area, matching the tables and chairs, giving the place an ambient, cosy feel.

Their table sat towards the back of the area, a booth-style seating with high enough backs on them they should block out some of the other people's conversations. They sat opposite each other, and the hostess asked for their drink order. Once they relaxed into their seats and the hostess had headed off to collect their drinks, Heath smiled at Rory.

"Have you been here before?"

Rory nodded. "I came with Carlton once a few months back but haven't been since."

"I've only been once, too. Last year with my brother."

"How is your brother?" Rory cocked his head to the side. "You don't talk about him very much."

Heath sighed and leaned forward, resting his crossed arms on the table. "He's doing good. Did I tell you his name?" At Rory's negative answer, Heath said, "Parker. He's a little shit sometimes."

"Is that not what younger siblings are always like?"

"Yeah, I suppose. Doesn't make them any more likeable, though." Heath chuckled. "Even now, when he's older, he still stirs up as much, if not more, trouble than when he was a teenager."

"My sister has calmed down a bit since she married, but she still enjoys winding me up. She is a Scot through and through, and I doubt she will ever change."

Heath was certain the tone of Rory's voice made it sound like his sister *should* change, but he didn't bring it up. "What's her name?"

"Aggie."

"How are your parents dealing with you being so far from home? If you don't want to discuss it, ignore me." Heath remembered Rory had shied away from talking about his reasons for being in Cambridge the last time they spoke about it.

"Tell you what, let's get some food on our plates, then we'll discuss my parents if you still want to know."

Heath agreed, and they ambled over to the buffet displays. There were several stations—four standalone warming counters: one had soups and breads, and three had a vast variety of Chinese foods to choose from. As he had been last time, the choices overwhelmed Heath.

"I never know what to choose," he mumbled.

"I always go half and half. I choose half a plate of things I know I like, then half a plate of things I've never tried before."

Heath slid his gaze to the side. "That's surprisingly sensible, Mr Stephenson."

"I have my moments."

Heath laughed at the haughty expression on Rory's face. When they made it back to their table, their drinks were waiting for them, and they dug in. Groaning as his taste buds flooded with flavour, Heath closed his eyes and savoured the moment.

"Why does food always taste better when someone else cooks it?" he asked.

When he received no reply, he lifted his gaze to Rory's, sucking in a breath at the heat simmering in his eyes.

8

# Rory

The sound coming from Heath had made Rory instantly hard, but he couldn't take his gaze from the man, even when Heath's eyes widened at whatever he saw in Rory's expression. There was no way he'd be able to leave Heath without a kiss tonight. He needed to feel those lips on his. He cleared his throat and broke their staring contest, focusing on his plate instead.

Inhaling and exhaling slowly, Rory ate a few more bites before Heath brought their conversation back to where it had been before.

"So, your parents?"

Rory sat back, trying to figure out where to start. "I love my parents, don't get me wrong. They are very set in their ways. My entire family is. How I turned out like I am, I'll never know. To them, the plan had always been for their children to find nice Scottish partners and then live happily ever after in the same city, bringing a large brood of kids into the family. Rinse and repeat for generation after generation."

"And you didn't want that?"

"I like the idea behind it. I didn't understand why the person had to be Scottish, why we would have to stay in Perth, or why we would have to have lots of kids instead of one or two. It was as if those were the rules, and they couldn't be broken." Rory sighed.

"Aggie is following the rules. She's married to a complete asshole who is cheating on her and has been for years. She refuses to see reason because she wants to make our parents proud." He huffed and shook his head. "She's determined to follow our parents' wishes, regardless of her own happiness. It was the reason I rebelled. Not when I was younger, about the dialogue thing, but about staying in Perth."

"You couldn't watch her hurting."

The way Heath stated the truth without it being a question made Rory realise he understood.

"It felt like she was settling for second best, and our parents don't care about her feelings. I didn't want that for me. I *couldn't* have that for me. I would've slowly died inside."

Heath reached forward and covered Rory's hand with his own. "You did the right thing."

"Did I?" It was a rhetorical question. Rory returned to eating and tried to change the subject. "I'm setting up a fundraising event for Spencer. I'm planning a New Year's Eve party at the shelter in one of the large barns behind the other buildings. Carlton and Emma have been organising the decorations, and I've tasked myself with finding a DJ and sorting the food."

"The owner agreed to it?"

Rory nodded. "Yeah. It took a bit of creative talking, but after telling him about Spencer and his potential medical bills, he was happy to give me a budget to use. Not much of one, mind you."

It had not surprised him that Mr Harding had given him a small budget, but Rory had not argued because the shock that the man had agreed to the fundraiser at all had rendered him speechless. Rory didn't care if he had to dip into his own money to pay for extra things if it meant the fundraiser was a success. Rory had also used the excuse that it was more advertising for the shelter; therefore, more money, too. He hated using the money the adoptions brought in as bait, but there had been no choice.

"That's fantastic. Make sure you give me some posters or flyers. I can have them at the reception desk at the clinic. I'll get Elaine to mention it to the clients."

"Thanks."

They finished their meal, swapping childhood stories, and they left after Rory paid, citing the fact that it was his turn. Heath hadn't liked it, but hearing Rory's tone, he knew it meant something to him.

"Do you like pantomimes?" Heath asked, out of the blue.

"I haven't been to one for years, but I think I would enjoy it. Why?" He slid his arm through Heath's, and they walked back towards Rory's car.

"The Snowman is playing at the theatre, and I thought it might be nice to see it."

"Sounds like a plan."

"I was thinking maybe one of the last shows, so you don't have to worry about it while you're thinking of the fundraiser. What do you think?"

Rory closed his eyes briefly and rested his head on Heath's shoulder, amazed by how thoughtful Heath was. Not that he'd never met thoughtful people before, but they had never pointed it in his direction to this extent. "That would be great."

A short while later, Rory stood in front of Heath on his doorstep, fingers gripping Heath's coat while Rory dragged him closer. Their lips met in a hurry, and Rory opened immediately. He held the back of Heath's head, his tongue sliding inside his mouth and exploring the wet heat. Not wanting to leave Heath with a rash on his face from his beard, Rory pulled back, pressing small kisses across Heath's face. He traced the freckles he couldn't see but knew were there.

"Kiss me, Rory," Heath pleaded.

"You'll get beard burn." As much as he worked to make his beard as soft as he could, it was difficult to stop it from irritating someone completely.

Heath pulled Rory closer. "I don't care. Kiss me."

Rory knew he shouldn't but was helpless to resist. He forged their mouths together once more, duelling their tongues, sucking on Heath's and biting at his lips. After several minutes, he pulled back, resting their foreheads together while they regained their breath. Lifting his head, he saw Heath's chin was already becoming red. He cupped Heath's chin.

"Be careful of your skin. It looks sore."

Heath's eyes sparkled, and he grinned. "I will."

"Goodnight, Heath."

"Night, Rory."

Rory pressed their lips together once more, then pulled away and headed to his car. If he hadn't left then, nothing would've stopped him from following Heath into his house. He was fast becoming addicted to this guy.

· • • ● • ● • ● • • ·

"Why didn't you tell me you were spending Christmas alone?"

Rory jumped and banged his elbow on the corner of the filing cabinet he'd been looking through. Rubbing it hard, he turned a pained gaze to Heath. "What?"

"Carlton told me you don't have anyone to spend Christmas with and that you've refused several people's offers to stay with them."

Rory rolled his eyes. "I'm an adult, Heath. I can make my own decisions regarding who I spend my time with. Christmas is not a big deal for me. I'm happy to spend it here with the dogs." It was true. Christmas had never been a large holiday for him since he'd grown up. His parents had insisted on his presence in Perth, but Rory had declined, saying no one could cover for him. A nice excuse, as far as he was concerned. They didn't need to know that he'd told everyone else to take the time off instead.

"Christmas is...huge, Rory!"

Rory smiled at Heath's enthusiasm. "Then enjoy it."

"I won't without you."

Rory stared at him, trying to find the underlying meaning behind his words. "Yes, you will. You have your parents and brother to spend time with. Go." He shooed Heath out the office door, intending to head to Carlton and give him a piece of his mind about tattling to Heath about his plans.

"No."

"What do you mean, no?"

They stood face to face, toe to toe, and Rory could see the determination in Heath's expression. "I would like you to spend Christmas with me and my family."

Rory narrowed his gaze. "Answer me a question. If you hadn't found out about me spending Christmas alone, would you have asked me?"

Heath flushed and rolled his lips inwards, an unusual show of...uncertainty, maybe. Rory frowned, trying to figure out what was going on. He heard Heath inhale and exhaled, then square his shoulders.

"Yes. If I had...not chickened out several times over the past couple of weeks, I would have."

Rory clenched his jaw against the need to smile at Heath's uncharacteristically shy demeanour, knowing Heath would get the wrong idea. "In that case, I would love to spend *some* of Christmas with you."

"Some?" Although Heath's eyes had lightened with his answer, he appeared wary of Rory's word use.

"Yes, some. I won't be there straight away. That is your time with your family. But I will join later if you would like me there."

Heath grinned and wrapped his arms around Rory. "Perfect, although you could come first thing too..." he said, pulling away.

"Don't push it." Rory failed to sound stern.

"All right."

"How is Spencer doing?" Rory changed the subject to the reason for Heath's visit. Spencer had appeared a little unstable on his feet for the past few days, and Carlton had requested Rory call Heath for another check-up.

"He's all right. He's losing muscle mass in his legs, which, unfortunately, is one of the symptoms. With degenerative myelopathy, there's nothing I can do for him, but once he learns to accommodate to the unfamiliar sensation, he'll hopefully perk up a bit more." Heath pulled Rory in for another hug. "I'm sorry I can't do anything else."

Rory rested his forehead on Heath's shoulder, breathing his scent in—soap and a hint of sweat—trying to work through what he knew would be a tough time. "It's not your fault. I just wish he could find a home with people who will love him despite all his health problems."

"Well, he's loved here. That's enough for now. He seems happy enough, usually. I know you'll be able to find someone for him soon."

"I hope so." Rory pulled himself together and pushed Heath away from him with a swat. "Anyway, get back to work, slacker."

Heath pecked his lips, then pivoted away, soft laughter drifting back. Rory couldn't keep the smile off his face.

# 9

# Heath

"Jesus, Heath. Sit down before you wear a hole in the carpet." His mother's voice whipped across the room, and Heath jumped.

"Sorry. I'm…"

"Excited. I know. I've not seen you this jittery since you brought home your first boyfriend at fifteen."

His mother, Grace, had always been the more laid-back of his parents. She was more than happy to take things as they come and not be too fussy about appearances. At sixty years of age, she showed no signs of slowing down, but then again, neither did his father at sixty-six.

The doorbell rang, and Heath raced to answer it, his brother's laughter following in his wake. Opening the door, he smiled at Rory, tucked up in his coat, hat, scarf and gloves.

"Come on in."

Rory stepped in. "Thanks. It's freezing out there."

"Heath, bring him in to say hello," his mother called.

Heath rolled his eyes and sighed. "I have my orders."

Rory smiled, unwrapping his scarf and removing his outdoor things. Once they hung with the rest, Heath leaned forward and brushed a kiss across his lips. He'd been waiting too long to do that. At least it felt like it.

"Merry Christmas," Rory whispered.

"Merry Christmas, sweetheart."

Reluctantly, Heath pulled back, knowing they would send Parker searching for them if they didn't appear soon, so he grabbed Rory's hand and started walking back to the living room.

"Oh, wait!" Rory let go and stepped back, snatching a large bag from the floor before returning to Heath's side.

"What'cha got there?" Heath glanced at Rory's flushed cheeks.

"I didn't want to come empty-handed."

"You didn't have to—"

"I know. I wanted to."

They entered the living room, where his mother sat in her usual armchair, knitting within reach, and Parker sprawled across the sofa. The room was the centre of their family life, a little old-fashioned in design but full of memories.

"Mum, this is Rory. Rory, this is my mum, Grace, and my brother, Parker."

"Nice to meet you," Rory said.

Grace rose to her feet, a little slower than she would've liked, Heath was sure, then came over and embraced Rory. "It's so nice to meet you, Rory. Thank you for sharing Christmas with us."

"Thank you for letting me be here." Rory reached into the bag when Grace released him. "I have some gifts. They're not much, but—"

"They will be perfect, I'm sure." His mother had a knack for making people feel comfortable and at home.

Rory gave the gifts to his mother and Parker, then passed Heath's to him. "I have one for your dad, too."

"He's just in the middle of checking the dinner, but he'll be back in a few minutes," Grace said, resuming her seat and resting the gift on her lap.

"Oh my god!" Parker's voice had Heath focusing on his brother. "You got me tickets for a home match?"

"Heath mentioned you liked football. If you don't like them, feel free—"

"You are awesome, man! I tried to get tickets and couldn't get any. How did you—"

"Parker! Don't go asking Rory to spill his secrets. That's rude."

"Sorry, Mum. Thanks, Rory. It's great."

Heath shook his head at the excitement vibrating through Parker that even Heath could feel as far away as they were standing.

"It's beautiful, Rory. Thank you so much."

Heath looked at the snow globe his mother had received, then glanced at Rory, seeing his cheeks flushed dark red. When Rory's gaze met his, he saw a light in his eyes. He turned his attention to his own gift, unwrapping it gently. It was heavy but small. When the paper fell away, he grinned. There in his hands was an ornament of a dog, the image of Spencer, and a small hedgehog. The dog was leaning down with his front legs flat and his bottom in the air and stared at the little spiky guy in front of him. It was so realistic.

Turning to Rory, Heath lifted his arm around Rory's shoulders and hugged him close. "Thank you," he whispered in his ear. "I love it."

"Ah, there you are."

Heath turned and saw his father enter the room. "Rory, this is my father, Bill."

Rory glanced at Heath, something flickering in his expression before he schooled it and held out his hand for his father. "Nice to meet you, sir."

"Now, now. No, sir, for me. Bill is just fine." Rory held out the gift he'd brought for his dad. "Why, thank you, son."

His father sank into the armchair next to his wife and ripped off the wrapping paper. Heath felt Rory fidgeting beside him.

"Heath mentioned you enjoyed fishing. If it's not the right one, you can change it," Rory said, wringing his hands.

"It's bloody perfect." His dad held up a small box of fishing hooks, immediately opening them to see what kind were inside.

Heath pressed a kiss to Rory's temple. "You're amazing," he said. Rory ducked his head.

The rest of the day passed by in a blur of eating, laughter and celebration. Rory had told him earlier that he would only stay for a couple of hours because he didn't want to intrude on his time with his family, but every time he mentioned leaving, Grace thought of another reason for Rory to stay for longer. Heath loved that woman.

By the time Rory deemed it necessary for him to leave, it was early evening, and they had fed him again, much to Heath's amusement. Heath left at the same time, wanting to give his parents a bit of a break from entertaining. He knew Parker would retreat to his man cave as soon as he was no longer needed for dishwashing, so it would give his parents some alone time to relax.

"Thank you for coming, Rory. It was so nice to see you." Grace embraced Rory once he had wrapped up, ready to face the cold weather.

"Thank you for having me, Grace."

Heath hugged his parents before they exited the house, and he walked Rory to his car. "Thank you, Rory."

"For what?"

"For being you. You are an amazing person." He wrapped his arms around Rory and drew him in for a kiss. Mindful of Rory's opinion to leaving beard burn on Heath, he kept it light, but he wouldn't for much longer. He wanted the evidence of their relationship on him, and he couldn't wait.

Before they went their separate ways, Heath just held Rory, despite how cold it was. He didn't want to let him go.

"So, your father...is he really called William Williams?"

Heath snorted when Rory's words hit him. "Yes. His parents were adamant they were going to name him after his great-grandfather. It was only after they registered him, they realised the issue, but by then, it was too late. His dad started calling him Bill instead, which negated some issues."

Rory pulled back, smiling. "I can imagine that is not the easiest of names to live with."

"Exactly." Heath studied the man who had come to mean so much to him. "Merry Christmas, Rory."

"Merry Christmas."

# 10

# Rory

Music blared from the speakers that had been set up in each corner of the barn, and Rory winced when the beat vibrated through him. "Danny! Turn it down a bit!" The volume reduced a little, making it bearable, but Rory would've preferred silence. He couldn't do that to the people who had come to support the shelter with their fundraising efforts, though.

He surveyed the area, seeing it teeming with guests, and acknowledged that it was a success. The party had started a couple of hours prior, and Rory had finally been able to sit down and check that everything was progressing as planned. Danny was in charge of the music—he hadn't realised the college kid who volunteered several times a week was a music student. That had been a fantastic find when Emma had told him. The other college volunteers, Skyler and Lia, plus Toby and Emma, were helping with making sure there were enough drinks and food on the tables and answering any questions anyone had.

They had decorated the barn within an inch of its life, and Angie had the idea to blow up pictures of all the dogs waiting to be adopted and pin them around the room. Rory had already had several requests to visit with dogs the following week. All in all, the fundraiser had been a success. They had raised enough money to cover what Mr Harding had given them for a budget and also a good amount for Spencer's medical care should he need it.

"It's going well, isn't it?"

"Did you think it wouldn't, Australia?"

Carlton chuckled. "I knew you wouldn't have it any other way, and neither would Heath."

Heath had sent several people from the clinic to Rory for tickets to the event, and he was grateful. He'd even bought tickets for his parents and Parker. The shelter had sold every ticket they'd made available. Apparently, people loved being fed, watered and allowed to dance to music. It wasn't Rory's idea of a good time, but everyone was different.

"What about you? Are you enjoying yourself, Carlton?"

Carlton sighed. "Would be better if I had someone to share it with."

Rory glanced over at him, seeing the shadows behind his eyes. "You will find someone, Carlton. Just be patient."

"Patience is not my virtue."

"Ain't that the truth." Nolan, one of the shelter's part-time employees, dropped into the seat next to Carlton, and Rory raised his eyebrows at the tension now visible in Carlton's body.

"I need to go check on..." Carlton didn't finish his sentence; he just stood and walked off.

Nolan sighed. "One of these days..."

Rory frowned. "One of these days, what?"

"I don't know how many times I've asked him out, but he refuses. If he truly wasn't interested, I would've given up, but I know he is."

"Why is he refusing, then?"

"I have no idea." Nolan shook his head. "Maybe I *should* give up." Nolan faked a smile. "I'll catch you later, Rory."

"See you." Rory watched as a dejected Nolan walked in the opposite direction to that which Carlton had gone. He hadn't caught any tension between the two of them before, but maybe it was because they only worked one shift together out of the entire week. Rory exhaled heavily.

"That was an enormous sigh."

He looked over and saw Heath dropping into the seat next to him. "Hey. Are your parents okay?"

"Yeah, they're good. I've seated them the furthest away from the speakers, but Dad has already danced once with Mum, so they're happy."

"I saw. They're spritely." Rory chuckled.

"Only when they have a couple of drinks in them." Heath grinned. "What was the sigh for?"

"Something is going on between Carlton and Nolan. I'd not noticed any tension between them before now—which goes to show how professional they both are—but it threw me, especially when Nolan said Carlton kept refusing his advances."

"Hmm. I'm sure they'll work it out."

"Rory! It's time."

Emma waved him over to the makeshift stage they had rented for the event, and Rory blew out a breath. "Wish me luck."

"Break a leg."

Rory narrowed his eyes at Heath. "If I do now, you're in big trouble, buster."

Heath chuckled when Rory walked away and climbed up, taking the microphone from Emma.

"Good evening, everyone!" He waited for the cheers and clapping to die down before he continued. "Thank you so much for your support. This has been an amazing evening, and I have to thank all of you for its success. We have raised enough money for what we intended," he paused for the renewed enthusiasm to quieten again, "and for a little extra for my alcohol fund." He winked through the laughter and said, "Only kidding. For those who haven't already approached me, can I just remind you that the photos on the walls are of the dogs who are ready for adoption? They come in all shapes, sizes and personalities. If you are interested, please let one of the staff members know, and we can arrange for you to visit. Having spent so much time around these dogs, I can assure you they are all fantastic companions. As a final note, I want to thank you one more time, and I hope you enjoy the rest of your night."

He left the stage to cheers and headed back towards Heath.

"You did well, and you didn't break a leg."

Rory grinned, then paused. "Come with me." He walked towards the exit, stopping once to tell Carlton that he was in charge for the rest of the night because Rory was going home. He didn't feel guilty because that had been the plan all along. Carlton knew Rory wouldn't stay the whole night, so he had offered to lock everything up once everyone had gone home. They would all tidy up the following day.

With Heath trailing slightly behind him, he aimed for home. When they entered, he closed the cold out and locked the door, turning to find a fire burning in Heath's eyes. It wasn't midnight, so the new year had not been rung in yet, but he couldn't wait for Heath any longer. He needed him, burned for him.

When he began to remove his clothes, he saw Heath swallow before doing the same. When Rory's shirt was unbuttoned, he stepped closer. "Make love to me, Heath."

Heath's eyes widened, and for a second, Rory wondered if he'd used the wrong wording. At least until Heath grabbed him and fused their lips, wrapping his arms tightly around Rory's body as if he never wanted to let go. Rory was good with that idea.

When Rory's ass met an obstacle, he ripped his mouth away, finding out Heath had backed him into the kitchen table. He gripped Heath's hand and dragged him towards his bedroom. As much as he didn't care where they made love, he wanted comfort.

Entering his room, he let go of Heath and began undressing hurriedly, wanting nothing more than to have his skin against Heath's. Heath's chuckle had him glancing up at Heath's amused expression.

"What?" He paused his actions.

"You're so cute when you're impatient."

"Shut up and get undressed," Rory ordered, though his voice came out decidedly less stern than he wanted.

"Yes, sir."

Rory waited until he was sure Heath was undressing before resuming his own disrobing until he was left in his boxers. He hesitated, not sure if it was too forward to remove them, so left them on, climbing onto the bed after pulling the covers down a little.

Heath apparently had no concerns because he removed everything, and Rory got a good look at Heath naked as the day he was born. He was a vision. He was not overly muscular, but he had a definition that spoke volumes of how he took care of himself. His freckles, Rory found, dipped way lower than his collarbone, covering his chest and arms as well. Heath had a sprinkling of auburn hair over his whole body, and Rory couldn't wait to find out whether it was as soft as it looked.

Crawling from the bottom of the bed, Heath moved forward until Rory had to lie back, caging Rory with his arms.

"You are fucking gorgeous, Rory," Heath whispered.

Rory felt his body heat at Heath's words, and he closed his eyes and breathed deeply. When lips touched his throat, he arched his head back, giving Heath more room. Rory slid his hands up Heath's arms, over his shoulders and down his back, feeling the very slight abrasion of soft hairs.

Heath's tongue trailed down Rory's chest, leaving goosebumps in his wake from the slight chill in the air. His mouth surrounded one of Rory's nubs, making Rory bow up when Heath sucked hard. Featherlight sensations skimmed over his other nipple from Heath's fingertips. Both together sent pleasure streaming down to his groin, stiffening his cock further until his boxers no longer contained it.

"That feels fucking amazing," Rory whispered and arched again, trying to get closer and further away at the same time.

Heath's swollen shaft rubbed against Rory's thigh while his hands travelled down Rory's sides to his hips. His lips followed, licking, sucking, nipping at Rory's skin as he descended. Heath wasted no time in pulling Rory's boxers off, then encircling his cock with his hand before peering up at Rory through his eyelashes. Heath parted his lips, and Rory's breath hitched in anticipation.

# 11

# Heath

When Heath needed more, he licked his lips and, holding the base in his hand, sank down, tonguing the underside as he went. Rory's taste went to his head, and he couldn't get enough. He lifted and dropped his mouth several times, eyes rolling in the back of his head at the taste. Rory's hands rested on his nape, nails digging in, but Heath didn't care.

For a last time, Heath swallowed him as far as he could and sucked hard on his retreat, Rory's hips following, then dropping to the bed. He crawled over Rory, covering his lips and transferring the taste to his mouth. Rory groaned and held him close, thrusting his hips against Heath's.

Pulling away, Heath cradled Rory's head and asked where the supplies were, grabbing them from the drawer Rory indicated after a few seconds of thought. Dropping the condom next to Rory's hips, he opened the lube, slicking his fingers before tossing the tube to the bed. He pressed against Rory's inner thighs, encouraging him to open to him fully, which he did. Heath groaned when it revealed Rory's puckered entrance. The need to get his cock inside this amazing man overran the need to put his mouth on him. He promised himself he would rim him one day soon.

Rubbing the slick over the tight opening, he massaged before pressing forward when Rory relaxed enough for the tip of his finger to enter. Taking it slowly, he prepared Rory, not wanting to hurt him even a little. Once Rory was trembling and lifting to meet the three fingers he'd put inside him, Heath pulled free, covering his shaft with the condom and slicking it quickly.

Heath rested a hand next to Rory's head, his other aiming his cock where it desperately needed to be. He paused, meeting Rory's pupil-blown gaze when his cock rested against the entrance. Rory seemed to understand his hesitation and nodded, gripping the sheets beneath him. Heath pressed forward, unwilling to thrust hard no matter how much he wanted to. Steadily, he gained entry until he was fully seated. He rested on his elbows, caging Rory in, then kissed him gently. When the kiss turned frantic, Heath withdrew and thrust several times. Not satisfied with the angle, he rose, tearing their lips apart, and gripped Rory's hips as he knelt.

Snapping his hips forward repeatedly yielded pleasure yet unintelligible sounds from Rory's mouth. Rory's cock looked an angry purple and was leaking precome like a tap leaked water. His hips drove into Rory's channel, the desire increasing with every plunge into his warm ass.

The incoherent mumblings continued when Rory wrapped his hand around his dick. Stroking himself in time with their thrusts had him coming in seconds. Rory's shout of completion and the squeezing of his muscles tipped Heath over the edge, and he slammed forward and held himself inside Rory as he came harder than he ever remembered coming before. He dropped onto his elbows, barely stopping himself from crushing Rory, and rested his head on Rory's heaving chest.

He gave himself a minute to recover, then held the condom while he withdrew, eliciting a whimper from Rory and a wince of sensitivity from himself.

Spying the bathroom from where he was sitting, he stood on shaky legs and washed up, bringing a cloth to clean Rory, who seemed unable to open his eyes.

"You okay there?" Heath whispered.

"Uh," was the only response he received.

He chuckled, taking the cloth back to the bathroom, then slid onto the bed next to Rory, pulling the covers up over them both, the chill in the air pebbling their heated skin. He rested his head on Rory's shoulder and laid his arm over his waist.

Rory cleared his throat. "That was..." he croaked, then fell silent again.

"It was," Heath agreed. "Get some sleep."

Rory brought his hand onto Heath's arm, squeezed but stayed quiet. Within seconds, Heath could hear small snoring sounds coming from Rory. He smiled, then joined him in slumber.

· · ● · ● · ● · ● · ● · ·

Heath had purchased tickets for the last show of the pantomime. He'd already cleared it with Rory because it had been on a Sunday, late afternoon, which was one of Rory's busiest days at the shelter, but he'd asked Angie to cover for him for a few hours. They had also invited his parents and Parker to join them.

They sat on the aisle seats around the halfway mark from the stage—Heath had it on good authority that they might get wet; therefore, he had gone with the safest bet. The pantomime was The Snowman, which he thought was very apt with the amount of snow they had received in the last couple of days.

As it took them through the story, jokes—good and bad—were plentiful, and everyone seemed in high spirits. The dancing between the Snowman and Father Christmas was beautiful to behold, a sensuality you wouldn't expect from a pantomime, but there, nonetheless.

"Do you think there is a relationship between those two?" he whispered in Rory's ear.

Rory tilted his head. "Probably," he replied. "Unless they are outstanding actors."

Heath pressed a kiss to his temple and linked their fingers.

Afterwards, Heath and Rory said their goodbyes to his parents and Parker, then wandered towards Heath's car.

"Did you enjoy yourself?"

"Very much. We'll have to do that every year." As if realising what he'd said, Rory cleared his throat and changed the subject, asking about the health of the other vet.

Heath grinned. "He's back to his old self, causing trouble wherever he goes."

"That sounds like him. Glad he's feeling better, though."

"Yeah, me, too. Despite him being a cantankerous old man, he's also a good guy underneath it all."

"I think he's very set in his ways and will be until he retires." Rory paused. "If he retires."

Heath laughed. "Yeah. I think he'd be happy working until the very end, but I don't think his wife will let him."

They climbed into Heath's car and sped towards Rory's house. That was where they had spent most of their time since the new year started, and Heath was more than happy with that. Rory had explained he needed to be on hand in case there were any problems with the dogs, and Heath had agreed. It didn't cause any problems for Heath; he could just as easily get to the clinic from the shelter as he could from his own home.

Occasionally, he had made moves to go home, but Rory had always invited him to stay. Heath had agreed, wanting nothing more than to spend more time with his boyfriend and get to know him better.

He also helped at the shelter when he could, above and beyond what his contract stated. He didn't mind. He loved the shelter as much as he loved the clinic.

He parked the car, turning off the engine, then glanced across at Rory, noticing his face had paled. Frowning, he reached for him. "What's wrong?"

Rory's attention was outside of the car. Heath followed his gaze to a larger car parked further away from the shelter's main building. Not recognising the vehicle, his hands moved to the keys, ready to start the car and get them away from whoever it was, but Rory spoke into the silence, "It's my parents."

# 12

# Rory

Rory couldn't believe his parents were there. Why hadn't they told him they were coming? He didn't want to get out of the car. As he'd told Heath before, he loved his parents, but they would not approve of anyone Rory was seeing unless that person fit in with his parents' stipulations. Heath did not. Rory would fight tooth and nail for them to accept Heath, but he was also tired of *having* to fight them. Why couldn't they be happy for him?

Blowing out a breath, he sent a small smile across to Heath. "I apologise in advance."

"You have nothing to apologise for."

"I will."

Heath frowned but followed when Rory exited the car. Rory didn't approach the other car; he led Heath to the entrance they used when the shelter was closed, knowing his parents would not be far behind. True to form, they entered, and Rory shut the door behind them, the automatic lock engaging. There was complete silence, except for their footsteps while he led the way to his home. He wanted nothing more than to reach for Heath, but he didn't want any kind of backlash to start before they were behind closed doors.

When they finally settled into the living room with hot drinks, Rory stood in front of them. "What are you doing here?"

"Is that any way to speak to your parents, young man?" His mother's voice whipped across the room, making him flinch.

"Mother, Father, may I introduce Heath? Heath, these are my parents, Mr and Mrs Stephenson." He didn't dare give Heath their given names, knowing he would receive another reprimand if he did.

"Nice to meet you both," Heath said with a smile, though Rory could see it was forced.

They didn't acknowledge him other than to look his way. Rory could feel his hackles rising. He didn't mind the treatment being aimed at him, but he would not put up with it being pointed at Heath. He was about to say something when his father stood up.

"Do you have space for us to stay with you?"

Rory did if he wanted to give up the use of his office. He refused, though. "No, sorry. It's not a big place." He refused to look at Heath when he spoke the white lie.

"I will call around for somewhere to stay." His father walked around the sofa.

"Would you like some help, Mr Stephenson?" Heath asked, also standing.

His father paused, staring at Heath, then nodded, and Rory let out a silent breath.

Heath winked as he walked past, following his father to the kitchen. Rory knew it was to give him some space with his mother, but he wished Heath had stayed. Then again, he also wished Heath had never had to meet his parents at all. He wouldn't wish it on his worst enemy. Not everyone could understand how they were brought up. A person had to live through it to understand what was going on behind the scenes.

"What are you doing with that boy?"

Rory wanted to laugh but knew he couldn't. What did she think he was doing with him? Swallowing his automatic response, he changed his wording and answered, "He's my boyfriend."

His mother stared at him, saying nothing. That stare was the bane of his existence, and he knew it could make him cave and give away every tiny little detail if he let it. He turned away, taking the seat Heath had vacated. The room that had been a warm, cosy sanctuary now felt like a cold, stiff prison. It was as if he was still at his childhood home.

"Aggie is pregnant again. You've hardly seen your nephew. Are you going to miss out on the next one, too?"

"I will see them." He refused to state when.

"I don't know why you moved so far away from us. The journey was far too long."

"Did you drive the entire way?"

"Don't be silly. We got a flight, then drove from the airport. I don't intend to do it very often, so make sure you come home, so I don't have to come here."

Rory refused to answer that. Heath chose that moment to come back into the room. Rory's brow creased at the tension running through his boyfriend. He stood.

"I have to head out."

Heath's voice was low, vibrating with something.

"What's wrong?" he echoed Heath's earlier question.

"Nothing." He glanced at Rory's mother briefly before returning to Rory. "I'll speak to you later."

Heath left without a kiss or any kind of proper goodbye. A stone set in Rory's stomach. "What did you do?"

"Nothing that shouldn't have already been done," his father said. "We have a hotel. Let's get settled in. We can speak to Rory tomorrow when he's more rested."

His mother obeyed his father as she always did. His father was a man of few words, but they meant more than any others put together in his parents' relationship. No matter what his mother thought or said, she would abide by her husband's wishes.

Neither said goodbye when they left, the door closing quietly behind them. Rory moved to the window, watching them wander down the path to the exit. One minute, he was enjoying his time with Heath, the next people surrounded him, then he was alone. He had no idea what had happened. Yes, he did. His parents happened.

What were they even doing there? They had gone to a lot of trouble to visit him, and it worried him he didn't know the reason. His parents did nothing without a good reason. Their reasons, unfortunately, were not always in line with everyone else's thoughts. It had always been the same. It was their way or the highway, and when Rory had chosen the highway...well, all hell broke loose.

Rory grabbed his phone, dialling Heath. It rang out several times before going to voicemail. Rory's heart raced before he realised Heath was probably still driving.

"Hey, it's me. Erm, they've gone to a hotel. So, I'm on my own again. I know you probably wanted to give me time with them, but if you want to come back, you can. Otherwise, I'll see you tomorrow?"

He didn't mean to finish the sentence with a question. He knew they would see each other because they had already made plans for Heath to visit to check over Spencer, but something was niggling at Rory. He had a feeling his father had said something to Heath to get him to leave but couldn't prove it. He should've warned Heath more than giving him vague answers to his questions about his family. Rory hadn't thought they would ever come to visit him, so he hadn't prepared Heath for their behaviour.

Hopefully, he wouldn't pay for that oversight.

He picked up the cups and piled them in the sink, ready for him to wash them in the morning. He didn't have the energy to do it then. He needed the obliviousness of sleep. It was the only way he could deal with what had happened. Tomorrow, he'd reach out to Heath again.

Rory slid into bed, placing his phone on the pillow next to him, close in case Heath called back. He stared at it, willing it to ring.

# 13

# Heath

Heath had promised himself he would not be a third wheel of a relationship. Rory knew what had happened with Alex and had agreed it was a shitty thing for a person to do. Rory's father had just proved how much Rory's words were just that.

Rory was fucking engaged!

Heath closed his eyes while hurt made it hard to breathe. He had believed everything Rory had fed to him. Every story of how his life had been in Perth. Every word against his parents. Jesus, Heath even had his own parents involved now. He didn't know how to break it to them about Rory's behaviour.

He had suffered through Alex's feelings towards another man for weeks before Alex finally broke it off. In hindsight, Heath should have done it way before then, but he had enjoyed being part of a couple. Obviously, he had buried his head in the sand again.

With everything that had happened with Marcus over Christmas—the mean, calculating person he had proven to be—Heath had no one to turn to apart from his family. His friends were through Marcus or through Alex, neither of whom was now part of his life. People he'd met through Rory would be out of reach, too. It left no one.

Heart heavy, he trudged up the stairs, ducking quickly into the shower to free himself from the scent of Rory. Luckily, they had never slept in his bed, so Heath should be able to sleep without smelling Rory on his bedsheets.

Lying on his back, letting the cool air pebble his clean, damp skin, his eyes stung and his head throbbed while he tried to sleep. Which he must've done because he awoke freezing cold and feeling like his head was stuffed full of cotton wool.

Checking the clock, he saw it was five in the morning. There was no point in him trying to get back to sleep because his alarm would go off in half an hour. He rolled onto his back and groaned at the soreness in his muscles. Dragging himself upright, he sat on the edge of the bed and reached for his phone, glancing around the room when it was not on his bedside table as it usually was. He must've left it downstairs.

The shower called his name, and he turned the temperature down to the coldest he could withstand. The burst of chilled water helped clear his foggy brain, and he finally remembered leaving his phone on the coffee table. After he dressed, he picked up his phone and headed to the kitchen. His phone had registered several missed calls, but he checked the messages first. All were from Rory. Not wanting to see what excuses he had come up with, Heath checked his call list, seeing all the calls were from Rory, too, with three voicemails. Turning off his phone, he left it on the counter and prepared his breakfast.

Once he'd eaten some fruit—because he hadn't been able to swallow the scrambled egg he'd made—he turned his phone back on because he knew his parents would worry if they couldn't get hold of him at any point. He just had to hope that there wasn't an emergency at the shelter because he wasn't sure if he could go there and pretend like everything was fine.

Not wanting to wallow any further, Heath set out for the clinic. There was plenty of work that he could do before the doors opened for clients.

• • • ● • ● • ● • • •

Being the first day open since before the new year, the day was crazy busy. Pet owners were turning up without having made appointments, but rather than turning them away, Heath told Elaine to ask if they'd be willing to wait. Some did, some didn't, but it made the day go by quicker. He'd barely had time to think about anything other than the people and animals in front of him at that moment.

Every time he had a spare minute, his brain went back to the previous night, and it took everything in him to stop himself from bringing his anger into the treatment room. He managed, though.

When the last client had left, Elaine locked the door and glared at him.

"What?"

"What the hell is going on?"

"What do you mean?"

Elaine crossed her arms. "What do I mean? You have spent ten hours running yourself ragged for no reason. What's going on?"

"Nothing's going on. I just want to keep busy. You know how much I hate turning people away. It all turned out okay."

"Okay?" Elaine paused, then placed her palms up towards him. "Do you know something, Heath? Go ahead and deny all you want that something is bothering you, but I know you. You are so stubborn sometimes. If you don't want to tell me, fine. You could've just said that. But ignoring whatever it is won't do any-thing." Elaine stalked around the desk, grabbed her things from the drawer and slipped her coat on, her bag held at her side. "I'll see you tomorrow."

Heath locked the door behind her, watching to make sure she got to her car before turning away. He dimmed the lights to show the clinic was closed, but he had no intention of leaving yet. There was plenty of paperwork to do.

After several hours, his head pounded, he had a crick in his neck, and his eyes were sore, but he'd made a dent in what needed to be done. Unwilling to go home, he headed to reception to switch the lights off completely, then returned to his office, laying himself on the sofa. He'd catch a few hours of sleep, then do some more work before the clinic opened.

Sleep didn't come, though.

Heath tossed and turned. One minute he was hot; one minute he was cold. He tried to divert his mind to happier things, but his mind kept replaying the words Rory's father had said.

*"Why are you even here?"*

*"I don't know what you mean, Mr Stephenson. I'm here because Rory wants me to be."*

*"How can you live with yourself?" Heath said nothing, not under-standing what the man was talking about. "Causing Rory to cheat on his fiance? You appeared to be a better man than that."*

*Heath froze. "You must have something wrong, Sir. Rory isn't engaged."*

*"He's been engaged for years, Heath."*

*"Why did he move away if he was?"*

*Rory's father sighed. "He wanted to spread his wings a bit. We thought if he had some time away from Perth, he would come back with renewed interest in staying in the city. If not, James would move here instead."*

*Giving the other man a name made Heath's heart sink as the truth weighed heavily on him. Rory's words about liking the idea of his parents' dream but not the execution flittered through his head. Rory obviously wanted James to move to Cambridge with him.*

*"Maybe you should leave. I can see this was a shock to you. I honestly thought you knew."*

*Heath gave a tight-lipped smile and headed to the living room to excuse himself from the rest of their planned evening.*

Heath decided he was extremely bad at choosing people—both friends and boyfriends, apparently. With everything that Marcus had done to Casey...well, Heath had never thought Marcus was capable of that, but as soon as Heath had found out, he cut Marcus from his life. He'd never support someone who not only backed an abuser but also threw bricks through people's windows when he didn't like who his ex-boyfriend was dating. Heath shook his head.

As for Rory...Heath should've known better. Why he thought people were nice and decent, he had no idea. From now on, he was staying away from relationships. He'd stick to working. At least here, he knew people wanted him for himself, not as a substitute.

If he could only tell his heart to stop pining for what he'd lost.

# 14

# Rory

Rory sat at his desk, head in his hands, still unable to believe what he had done that morning.

*His parents entered the house once Rory unlocked the door, his mother bustling in with food as she normally would, his father following more sedately with the paper in his hand.*

*"Good morning, sweetheart. Did you sleep well?"*

*Rory had no idea what she was playing at. "Not really. I thought we were meeting for lunch?"*

*"Well, I saw how bare your cupboards were yesterday, so thought I'd bring you some breakfast instead." She busied herself in his kitchen, and Rory stood watching the whirlwind that was his mother.*

*"What happened with Heath yesterday?" Rory turned his attention to his father, who sat at the table and opened his paper.*

*"He helped me find a hotel."*

*"And?"*

*"Then he said he needed to go home."*

*"Well, that's hilarious because before you arrived, we had plans. I doubt very much that he would leave without explaining unless something else happened."*

*"What are you insinuating?" his mother said, pausing with a pan in her hand.*

"I'm not insinuating anything. I'm asking you outright what you said to Heath to make him want to leave."

"I don't like what you are implying, Rory. You would never have taken this tone with us before."

Rory shook his head. He'd been over their visit a thousand times during the night and had come to only one conclusion...his father must have said something to Heath. Unable to stay in their presence for a moment longer, he stormed out of the house with his mother calling his name from behind him. He didn't stop until he neared the entrance to the shelter, at which time his arm was caught, and he was spun around to face his father.

"What do you think you are doing?"

"I'm going to work. When I finish work, I would very much like neither of you to be here." He turned, ready to walk away again, but his father stopped him.

"Do not turn your back on us...for him."

Rory saw red. He wrenched his arm out of his father's grip, liking the surprise etched on his face. He turned his gaze to his mother, making sure both could hear him. "I would turn anyone away for him. He is worth more than all of you put together."

His mother slapped him, and Rory licked the corner of his mouth, tasting copper. "I will not have my son talk to his parents like that."

"You are not my parents!"

"Yes, we are, and we are taking you home with us, now." His father tried to grab his arm, but Rory danced out of reach.

"I'm going nowhere with you."

"You have a fiancé in Perth, waiting for you to return home."

"What the hell? You know I was never engaged to any...That's what you told him! You told him I was fucking engaged? No wonder he ran out of here as fast as he could!"

"Keep your voice down."

"No, I will not."

*"I told him the truth. You are engaged and have been since before you were born."*

*Rory laughed, a little maniacally if he heard right. "See, this is why I left. You have to force everyone to bend to your will. Why not just let us live our lives?"*

*"You have no clue how to make your life the best it can be."*

*"So, instead, you tell Aggie to lie to her boyfriend about being pregnant, so he'll marry her? How is that giving her a better life? She hates it."*

*"Don't be silly. She's happy."*

*"Happy! She's living a lie, and now you want me to do the same! It's not happening. Ever. I am not and will never be engaged to a person of your choice. Now that we have cleared that up, leave. I do not want to see you again."*

*He turned and stalked away.*

*"You do this, and you'll regret it," his father called to him.*

*Rory pivoted around. "This is something I should've done years ago. The only thing I regret is that it took me so long to realise how unstable you both are and how in love with Heath I am."*

After that, he had locked himself in his office and stayed away from everyone. Carlton found him at the end of the day, though Rory had to get up to unlock the door for him.

"Everything okay?"

"I've been better." Rory cleared his throat. "How's everyone doing out there? Sorry I haven't been around."

"Don't worry about it. We know what we have to do, and there are plenty of staff around. My concern is you. You've never locked yourself away before."

Rory stared at the papers on his desk, eyes unfocused. "My parents told Heath I was engaged to someone from Perth."

"What? Why would they do that?" Carlton sat in the visitor's chair.

"They had arranged it before I was even born." Rory scoffed. "It wouldn't surprise me one bit if it had been."

"You obviously told them no. So, what's the problem?"

Rory swallowed hard. "Apparently, I was the only one who believed enough in us to fight because I rejected my parents for him. Since I've been in here, I've been trying to figure out why Heath didn't even ask me if it was true. He just left. No fighting for us, no trying to find out the truth. He walked out without a word." Rory continued in a whisper, "I'm in love with him, and he left."

Carlton moved next to him and put an arm around his shoulders. "Maybe he's been trying to figure it all out in his head. Sometimes, when things get thrown at you like that, your head gets messed up. Maybe he needed that time to make sure he was doing the right thing? I'm not saying he was right to leave, but maybe in his head it was?"

Rory shook his head. "I have to get back to this paperwork."

Carlton removed his arm and stood from where he'd crouched. "All right. You know where I am if you need me."

Rory nodded once. When the door closed behind Carlton, Rory slumped back in his chair. What a great way to figure out you loved someone...when they had already turned their back on you. He exhaled loudly, then leaned forward, intent on getting some more paperwork finished before he crawled into bed.

He never made it to bed. He woke with his face stuck to his hand, which, in turn, stuck to the papers beneath him. Sitting upright, he groaned as pain streaked down his spine. Sleeping at his desk was not good for his body. He stood on shaky legs, rounding the desk to exit the office. As he opened the door, he saw the lights were off, except for a few, which lit the way through the building. Rory headed to the reception area, checking the desk for where they left notes if something needed to be passed on to anyone.

Rory saw a note from Carlton saying everything had gone fine and that he'd locked everything up. He really needed to give Carlton a pay rise.

Checking the clock, he realised he'd slept for around five hours—no wonder his back was hurting. After nipping into the staff bathroom, he double-checked they had locked everything, then headed back to his office. He was no longer sleepy; therefore, he could do some more work.

# 15

# Heath

As Elaine locked the door, Heath slid down the wall to the floor, finally feeling the exhaustion in his body. "Rory's an asshole."

"What! Why?" Elaine walked to the seat opposite where he was and sat.

"His parents turned up at the weekend. His father told me the truth about Rory."

"What truth?"

"He's engaged to someone in Perth."

Elaine's expression, under other circumstances, would've been hilarious, but Heath felt nothing, only numbness. "There must be some mistake."

"No. According to his father, they were engaged before Rory moved here and have been in a long-distance relationship since."

"I can't believe it, Heath. Did you talk to Rory about it?"

He shook his head. "What was there to say?"

"Did he deny or acknowledge it at least?"

"I didn't ask."

Elaine narrowed her gaze at him. "Do you mean to tell me you took his father's word for it without confirming it with Rory?"

Heath fidgeted under her gaze but said nothing.

"Heath!"

"I didn't want to see the confirmation that I'd been dumb enough to fall for it again, all right!" Heath stood, pushing away from the wall and storming down the corridor to his office. He slammed the door, barely stopping himself from breaking down. Deep breaths counteracted the need to cry, at least for the time being. He knew he'd wanted to ask for her advice, but he hated being called out for his behaviour when it wasn't his fault.

Heath didn't know if he was grateful that Elaine had left him alone or not, but when the door finally opened, he hadn't expected to see Carlton.

"Everything okay? Are the dogs all right?"

Carlton nodded, frowning at him. "Yeah. They're all good."

"What?"

"Why haven't you responded to Rory's messages or calls?"

Heath turned his back, anger coursing through him. "He's sent you as his messenger, has he?"

"No. He doesn't even know I'm here. He's been dealing with a lot of shit the shelter has thrown at him and his parents, unfortunately. I wouldn't wish them upon my worst enemy."

"At least they're truthful."

"Are they? Could've fooled me." Heath could hear Carlton's steps around the small room. "Last I heard, they told their daughter to pretend to be pregnant so the father would marry her. Don't know how truthful that is."

Heath had known nothing about that. "Who told you that?"

"No one. I overheard Rory when he was yelling at them."

Heath's heart raced. Why had Rory been shouting at his parents? He didn't want to ask, even though he wanted to know the answer.

"Good thing, they went home the following day."

"I thought they were staying for a week. That's what his father said."

"Rory kicked them out."

Heath spun on his chair so fast he nearly fell off. "What?"

Carlton stared at him. "You tell me something." Heath inclined his head. "What made you leave?"

Heath licked his lips. He didn't want to cause animosity between employees, but he had once considered Carlton a friend. "His father told me about Rory's engagement. I'd already had someone play me for a fool once; I won't stand for it again." He turned back to this desk.

"Fair enough. One thing before I go...Make sure you're correct about which person is playing you for a fool, Heath."

Heath turned to answer, but Carlton had already shut the door. Shaking his head, he returned to his work, despite needing to sleep.

• • • ● ●•● ● • •

Several hours later, he woke to his phone ringing. Lifting his head, he put it to his ear and mumbled a greeting.

"Heath! There's something wrong with Spencer."

Rory's voice filled his ear—and his heart if he was truthful—and Heath was instantly awake, his vet instincts sharp.

"What's wrong with him?"

"He's struggling to breathe. I don't even know why I checked on him so late, but when I got to him, he was making this weird noise. Listen."

A wheezy sound came from the line, and Heath assumed Rory had placed the phone closer to Spencer. It was a little concerning, but knowing how the degenerative myelopathy worked, it was not uncommon. He couldn't rule out that it was something else, though, so he'd need to check.

"All right, Rory," he said when Rory came back on the line. "I'll be there shortly. Will you be able to let me in?"

"You can let yourself in. Everything is still the same," he whispered.

Heath swallowed hard at the reminder of what they'd had. "Okay. I'll be there soon." He hung up and raced to his car, barely remembering to lock the clinic first. Hands shaking when he started the engine, he prayed there was nothing else wrong with Spencer.

The journey didn't take as long as usual, Heath probably driving faster than the speed limit, but he didn't want Rory left alone with Spencer for too long. He knew how important these dogs were to the man. And to him. After he parked the car, he grabbed his bag and entered through the 'after-hours' gate, locking it behind him, then let himself through the side door to the shelter. Trying to be as quiet as he could so he didn't disturb the dogs too much, he wandered down the kennels until he reached Spencer's.

The door was closed, so Heath knocked quietly, then opened it, blinking at the brighter light inside the roomy space. When his eyes adjusted, he saw Rory sat with his back against the wall, legs stretched out, and Spencer cuddled into his lap, his head on Rory's chest.

"Hey," Heath said quietly. He knew Rory had seen him, but he didn't want to spook Spencer if the dog hadn't noticed him enter. Closing the door behind him, he stepped forward on soft feet and sat in a cross-legged position next to Rory, close enough to touch but not actually touching. "I'm going to listen to his chest, Rory." Rory nodded. Heath could see the pain etched into Rory's features. Despite what was going on between them, Heath's heart wrenched at the sight.

Ignoring his need to comfort, Heath concentrated on checking over Spencer. Apart from his laboured breathing, the dog seemed fine. Spencer had no signs of a cold or anything that would alert Heath to a problem.

"Spencer is doing okay, Rory. The breathing appears to be related to his illness, although I will monitor him over the next few days, just to make sure. There are no other symptoms to suggest anything major is wrong with him other than what we know already. I'm sorry, but he will be fine."

He moved to sit with his back against the wall, copying Rory's position but left a gap between them. They sat in silence for several minutes. Heath wondered whether Rory would prefer him to leave, but he didn't want to desert Rory and Spencer. It wasn't fair to either of them—Rory or Spencer—for Spencer to be going through this, and it didn't sit well with Heath to leave Rory alone with it.

As uncomfortable as the silence was, he'd take it over being abandoned any day. Which, he supposed, was what he had done to Rory...abandoned him to his parents. That wasn't particularly fair of him, especially because he knew how much Rory didn't like them, or so he thought.

Everything was muddled up, and Heath didn't know how to sort it all out. He preferred things to be straightforward; it saved on misunderstandings. Unfortunately, it seemed there might have been one—or several—between him and Rory. How did he bring up his own shortcomings without getting defensive, which was his default when he was in the wrong? If he was in the wrong.

He couldn't stop the back and forth he kept doing, unable to decide who was in the right and who wasn't. They needed to have a conversation about it, but he didn't think this was the time. As he opened his mouth to say something benign and uninteresting to fill the silence, Rory beat him to it.

"He doesn't even flinch when I touch his feet any longer."

The small, pained voice broke Heath's heart, and he knew right then that they needed to talk about what happened, especially with how deeply Rory felt things. He planned to do it the following day, after having slept.

Clearing his throat, Heath said, "It's the numbness he'll be experiencing. It's another reason his gait is uneven. He's losing muscle mass, but also the feeling in his feet, so he doesn't react as he would've before." He hated being the bearer of bad news, but things would be difficult for Spencer now. The little guy was charming and happy enough for it not to bother Spencer much, and he was adapting well to the issues he faced.

"I know how that feels," Rory said, a tear rolling down his cheek.

# 16

# Rory

Rory had been trying to withhold his tears, but the hopelessness he felt—about Spencer and his relationship with Heath—was pushing down on him, an almost physical pressure. Maybe he wasn't as numb as he'd thought.

When an arm came around his shoulders, he braced to push it off, but he needed it. So, despite the urge to yell and scream at Heath for leaving him, he rested against Heath and took comfort while he held the little dog who had come to mean so much to him. Spencer had settled down again and was breathing deeply, if still a little wheezily, indicating he was sleeping. It wasn't comfortable on the floor, but he couldn't bring himself to leave right then.

Rory tried to get hold of his emotions, tried to sort through them and figure out where his head was, but it was too much to handle.

• • • • ● • ● • • •

He woke, surrounded by the smell of dogs and warmth, except for his ass, which was smarting from the cold cement and having sat for so long. Rory blinked his eyes open, seeing dim light shining through the window, making it known it was early morning. Lifting his head, he cursed quietly when his neck protested loudly at the position he tried to force it into. Sleeping upright was not conducive to a good night's sleep.

Within those few seconds, he realised he was resting against Heath. The scent of him wrapped around Rory as much as any other, and he tensed and gently pulled himself away.

Heath stirred, groaning. At any other time, that would've been a good thing but not then. Rory didn't want to chance that Heath would want to dissect their relationship when Heath was so happy to walk away without a word. He'd only called him last night because he'd panicked and didn't know what to do. If he'd been less worried, he might have called someone else.

He stood, gently dislodging Heath's arm from around him while he cradled a sleepy pug in his arms. Spencer snuffled closer into him when Rory tried to settle him on his bed right next to his large red soft toy, making Rory smile, his heart easing more when Spencer's breathing wasn't as laboured or wheezy as the previous night.

Rising from his crouch, he turned, seeing Heath staring at him. Rory looked away and headed to the door of the kennel. By the strength of the light in the sky, there wouldn't be much time before staff started arriving, so he needed to get things sorted, the main thing being writing up what had happened with Spencer, but he couldn't close himself inside his office with Heath there.

He exited, and Heath caught the door before it closed behind him. Choosing to ignore his shadow, Rory headed to the supply store, greeting the dogs as he passed. He grabbed the wooden trailer, which they used to transport the containers of food, and began dividing food into the three smaller containers, ready to share between the dogs for their breakfast. Usually, Carlton would've done it, but Rory needed to keep himself busy.

Once the containers were full, he grabbed the handle of the trailer and pulled it towards the kennels. The cacophony of barks that met him had him grinning at the dogs' exuberance. They knew what time it was; well, they knew what was happening when the trailer came along, if nothing else.

"All right, all right. Hold your horses."

He'd barely fed a third of them before Carlton joined him, giving him a pointed look.

"I would ask if things were better, but the look on both of your faces explains everything," Carlton said.

Rory glanced at Heath, who was resting back against the wall with his arms crossed, bag at his feet and a mutinous expression on his face. Turning back to his job, he murmured, "Not sure what we can say at this point."

They worked side by side, Rory catching Carlton up on what happened with Spencer and believing that Heath would give up and leave because Rory was taking so long. When they'd finished, Heath was still standing there.

"Talk to him." Carlton pushed at Rory's shoulder.

"Who's the boss here?" Rory glared playfully.

"Me if you don't get your head on right." Carlton side-stepped Rory's backhand with a laugh and walked off.

Staring at Heath for a moment, Rory hustled towards the office, the chill of the morning working its way through his clothes because he hadn't put on a coat. It wasn't long before Heath was beside him.

"Are you not going to talk to me?" Heath asked, entering the main building.

Rory refused to peek at him. "Like you talked to me?" He knew it was a low blow, but he couldn't help the anger that bled into the words, sharp like the tattoo of his steps on the floor while he weaved through the maze towards his work haven.

"I deserved that."

Rory opened the door, leaving it wide like he did every morning before settling himself in his creaky chair, pointedly ignoring Heath, and switched the computer on. He could easily use the papers on the mahogany desk as a diversion, but he found himself curious about what Heath wanted, though he didn't show it.

"I'm sorry."

Rory sighed. "What are you sorry for?" He needed to know why Heath was sorry because, to him, it mattered. There could be different answers to that question, and Rory knew which answer he wanted. Only time would tell if Heath knew which answer was the most important.

"I should've asked you if what your father said was true before assuming it was, but I was scared of the answer."

Rory released some of the tension in him at Heath's answer, the one he wanted. It wasn't enough, though. "You need to trust me. Trust us. I did." Rory took a shaky breath. "I don't know if I can get back to that. You broke that bond, and I don't know how to fix it."

He watched Heath swallow hard and stare at the floor before meeting Rory's gaze again. "I'm trying. I'm sorry. I don't know how to fix me," he whispered.

Rory closed his eyes, trying to hold back the tears on Heath's behalf. He stood, rounding the desk, and stopped in front of Heath. "You're not broken, Heath."

"I am. You're an amazing, selfless, perfect guy, and I still believed what they said rather than trusting what I thought we had." Heath's voice was hoarse, pained even.

Cupping Heath's cheeks, Rory brought Heath's focus to him. "You've been hurt. It's understandable, but we need to get you over what Alex did. Otherwise, this will become a constant issue between us."

"We?" The hopeful note was hard to miss.

Rory gave a small smile and nodded. "We."

Heath slid his arms around Rory's waist, tucking his face into Rory's neck. Initially, Rory tensed, then settled, relaxing and closing his eyes while he wrapped Heath tight. He inhaled Heath's scent, the mixture of sweat and the leftover woodsy smell of his cologne. The same scent that remained on the pillow Heath had used for several nights.

They stayed that way for a few minutes, Rory basking in what he knew he'd missed but had refused to acknowledge.

Things would not be easy between them, but hopefully, by talking things through, they were on the way to being mended. Rory hadn't lied when he said he didn't know how to fix things. They would have to work together and figure things out along the way. He just hoped his parents would stay out of his life now. They had caused enough upset to last Rory's lifetime, and he didn't want any more. He wanted smooth sailing from now on.

Heath pulled back, eyes appearing slightly damp. "I am sorry."

Rory smiled. "I know."

Closing the distance between them, Heath moved slowly, obviously waiting to see if Rory would object to a kiss. He wouldn't, but he could understand Heath's hesitation. Rory moved forward, pressing their mouths together. It wasn't a kiss full of fireworks and electricity but one of healing. A promise of things to come.

When they pulled apart, Rory held Heath's face again. "We both need to learn to trust again."

# 17

# Heath

He'd also continued to help at the shelter when Rory needed an extra pair of hands but had stepped back from being there too much. Heath was continually aware of what he was doing so he didn't overwhelm Rory.

Having just finished at the shelter, he drove to his parents' house. They had not invited him for dinner, but he wanted to see them after having not seen them for a week. When he parked on the road in front of their house, he blew out a breath, trying to steel himself against the questions he knew his mother would ask about Rory. He'd not told her what had happened with Rory's parents, not wanting to see the reprimand in her eyes, but maybe it was time.

The car door opened, and Parker dropped into the seat. "Mum says, 'Are you coming in, or are you waiting for it to snow?'"

Heath chuckled. "I get it. I'm coming."

They both exited the car, Heath locking it behind him, then they trudged up the driveway and into the warmth. His parents' house was always warm because of his mother's poor circulation and arthritis.

"Good afternoon, sweetheart. How are you?" His mother folded him in her arms, and he held her tight, breathing in her cinnamon scent. She always reminded him of a bakery when he first entered, and the smell teased the senses.

"I'm good. Sorry I didn't mention I was coming."

"Don't be silly. There is always room for one more." She peered at him. "Or two more." Heath ducked his head. She patted his cheek and whispered, "Later." He nodded, knowing his time was up.

He spent a very enjoyable couple of hours catching up with them and helping clean up after dinner, then his dad and Parker left the kitchen, leaving Heath and his mother. He knew she would've orchestrated it, but he still had no idea what to say.

His mother made a cup of tea for her and a coffee for Heath, then sat next to him at the table. He wrapped his hands around the extremely hot mug, but the heat was welcome. Staring at the wisps of steam, he waited for the first question, which wasn't long in coming.

"What's happened?"

Heath sighed and rolled his lips inwards. "I messed up." Grace said nothing, and he knew it was because she wanted him to choose what he told her. His throat closed, and he couldn't say a word.

"Did you know that when you were younger, you were a social butterfly? You loved being with other people and hated being alone, even at home. You rarely stayed in your bedroom when you'd finished your homework. You preferred being with me or your dad, and then when Parker came along and was older, Parker, too." She sipped her tea. "I used to worry about you because you'd keep friends around even if they weren't the best influence. You were stubborn to a fault and believed everyone was a pleasant person." She sighed. "At least until they proved you wrong. And people did, repeatedly."

Heath hadn't remembered that.

"The same thing happened with Alex. Although a slightly different situation. You knew you should let go, and you refused, didn't you?"

Heath bobbed his head, knowing she spoke the truth as hard as it was to hear. "I knew the minute I saw him with Craig, but I believed him when he said there was nothing between them. Technically, it was true. Alex broke it off with me before he started seeing Craig."

His mother nodded. "Yes, although Alex should've never started a relationship with you when he was in love with someone else, you can't fault him for not cheating on you." She rested her hand over Heath's. "I never met Alex. I think that says something, doesn't it?"

"What do you mean?"

"Well, you brought Rory over for Christmas. A time usually put aside for family. Whereas Alex, I hadn't met at all. What do you think that means?"

Heath thought about his actions and realised what point his mother was trying to drive home. "I knew Alex wasn't right for me."

"Correct. Even though he hurt you, you were already bracing yourself for it not to last. Rory, on the other hand..."

She didn't finish her sentence and didn't need to.

"I made a mistake, and I hurt Rory." Heath swallowed some coffee, trying to delay the inevitable disappointment he knew she would feel. "His parents came to visit a couple of months ago unexpectedly. Rory's father told me Rory was engaged to someone in Scotland and had been for years." He closed his eyes and shook his head. "I believed him. I was so angry at Rory, so I left there and then. I couldn't face the knowledge that he had lied to me."

"But you hadn't been." A statement, not a question.

Heath laughed without humour. "How could you see it but not me? It took Elaine and Carlton, one of Rory's co-workers, for me to realise I'd made a mistake. I'd never even asked Rory for his side of the story. I'd just assumed and left him to deal with his parents alone. Even after everything he'd told me about them." He stood, marching over to the window and staring out at nothing. "Rory doesn't know if we can mend the relationship, but we're trying."

"Heath, you need to go back to being your younger self. Go back to believing the best in people. If they end up showing their worst, brush them aside but give them the benefit of the doubt. Like you did with Marcus."

Heath flinched at the reminder. "He's not a nice person."

"But he was to you. Yes, he showed his true colours towards others, and I wholeheartedly agree that you were right to cut him out when your beliefs didn't hold true with his. You cannot go into a relationship—any kind of relationship—without hoping this one is supposed to be part of your life. It's part of life. Now, you just need to find that younger self's belief and bring it back."

"But how can I trust people?"

"What's the phrase...innocent until proven guilty? It doesn't just relate to the law."

Heath placed his hands on the edge of the counter and hung his head. "I go into every relationship expecting it to turn bad. I never realised I did."

"That's your unconscious mind for you."

His mother shuffled over to the sink, rinsing their cups under the tap before leaving them in the sink.

"Thank you."

"You're very welcome, dear. Now, go find your man." Grace tilted her face to Heath, and he reached down and pressed a kiss to her cheek.

"Love you, Mum."

"Love you, too, sweetheart."

After saying a quick goodbye to his dad and Parker, he drove back to the shelter. Knowing Rory, he would still be at work, doing paperwork because it was only around half-seven in the evening. Despite their agreement that they were going to try again, Heath realised he had been holding back, waiting to get hurt again. Rory had never hurt him; in fact, it had been the other way around. Heath had been the one throwing all the punches at Rory, and that wasn't fair.

If their relationship was going to survive, Heath had to throw everything into it, and if he got hurt in the end, so be it. He refused to allow his past to ruin his future, and he wanted Rory to be his future.

It was time to make it up to his boyfriend, and he knew just how to do it. Heath had to hope he was not too late to fix what he had broken.

18

# Rory

R ory was fed up with how things had been going with Heath. He was fed up with the tiptoeing around each other they had been doing. There was no way they could fix what was wrong carrying on as they were. So Rory had a plan. He needed to get everything set up, and then he'd send Heath a message, asking him to come over.

Locking up his office, he wound his way through the barren buildings and outdoor area until he found himself in front of his door. Excitement coursed through him at what he was going to do...seduce his boyfriend. It seemed silly when he put it that way, but he needed to do something to get them out of the rut they'd dug themselves into.

He took a shower, then dressed in pyjama bottoms before tidying his bedroom a bit. Although Heath had been to his house in the last few weeks, he had not entered his bedroom since before Rory's parents had visited.

Brushing his parents aside, which was getting easier since he hadn't heard from them, Rory put on some 'mood' music and lit a few candles he'd found in the kitchen drawers, placing them around the bedroom. He dimmed the living room light, then grabbed his phone.

He had just pressed send when there was a knock at the door. Rory's heart leapt, and he knew it was Heath, meaning Heath had come back of his own volition. He raced down the stairs and took a breath before opening the door.

Heath stood there, eyes bright with a tentative smile, and Rory couldn't resist. He grabbed a handful of Heath's coat and dragged him over the threshold, fusing their mouths. The chill of the night had left its imprint on Heath's coat, but it only cooled Rory a little with how hot he was running. Heath's arms encircled him, the cold embracing him, too, but soon the temperature rose, and their mouths demanded from each other.

Rory reached between them to unzip Heath's coat and push it off his shoulders, letting it drop to the floor with a thump. They stumbled backwards as they both fought to divest Heath of his clothes until he wore his boxers with Rory still in his pyjama bottoms. Rory pulled back, locking gazes with Heath. He nudged their noses together and shared small kisses, never losing eye contact.

He felt it when Heath's patience snapped. Heath lifted Rory, who wrapped his legs around Heath's waist, and stumbled up the stairs, more so every time Rory licked at his lips. It wasn't the best idea when Heath was carrying him, but he couldn't help touching him. They staggered to Rory's bed, Heath dropping him to the mattress and covering him with his body. Their lips met in a frenzy, tongues tangling, their lower bodies thrusting against each other, their fabric-covered cocks sliding deliciously.

Rory's hands smoothed down Heath's back and into the waistband of his boxers, pushing them down with one hand and using the other to squeeze the globes. Heath twisted, earning groans from Rory, and removed his boxers, allowing Rory to use both hands against his pebbled skin. Running his fingertips back along Heath's spine, he felt Heath arch into him and his breath catch.

Heath reached down and hooked Rory's pyjama bottoms under his balls, so his cock sprang free. He hissed as his shaft slid against Heath's, their precome slicking their path. Rory's hand gripped Heath's ass again, grinding himself against Heath, his legs on either side of Heath's hips. Their lips met again, and Heath wrapped a hand around their dicks, groaning into Rory's mouth when they both thrust through the fist he'd made.

Heath tore his mouth away and kissed his way down Rory's neck to his nipple. He licked around the nub before flicking his tongue fast over the peak repeatedly, sending arrows of pleasure straight to Rory's groin.

Rory's hips jerked wildly, but he didn't want to come like that. "Wait," he panted. "Heath, hold on."

Heath pressed a closed mouth kiss to his nub, then raised his head, looking thoroughly pleased with himself.

"I need you inside me."

Heath kissed him, then rolled off, crawling to the bedside table for supplies. While he did that, Rory slipped off his pyjama bottoms and moved up the bed. He knew exactly how he wanted Heath. When Heath turned back with the lube and condom, Rory said, "Sit with your back against the headboard." Heath's eyebrows rose, but he did as Rory instructed.

Rory straddled Heath's legs, facing the bottom of the bed, his back and ass facing Heath. He looked over his shoulder, watching Heath's eyes darkened. "Get me ready. I need you."

Heath swallowed and licked his lips before nodding. Rory had always wanted to try this position. When a finger began teasing his hole, Rory pressed back, wanting more. His mouth went dry, and his head dropped when Heath's finger slid into him, and pleasure tingled up his spine. Heath gripped Rory's hips when two fingers entered, holding him steady as they slicked his insides and stretched him. At three fingers, Rory was pleading with Heath and pushing back, needing it harder, faster...just more.

"Fuck, Rory. You should see yourself. Open and fucking sexy."

Rory distantly heard a wrapper and the click of the tube, and then pressure at his entrance. He braced his arms and pushed back and forth until Heath was seated. Wanting to prolong the experience, Rory lifted off his hands and sat upright, Heath nudging further inside on a moan. Heath wrapped his hands around Rory's chest, and Rory turned his head, seeking Heath's mouth. Neither could move easily in this position, but that had been Rory's plan.

"God, I love the feel of you deep inside me." Heath moved, and Rory's breath hitched. He rotated his hips a little, making them both moan. "Oh, god!" Rory fell forward onto his hands, Heath's hands returning to his hips.

Rory slid off Heath's cock slowly, biting his lip when he felt his shaft dragging against his insides. Heath stopped his forward movement and yanked him back, embedding himself once more.

"Oh, fuck," Heath murmured.

Rory glanced over his shoulder, noticing Heath's focus was on where they joined. He was sure it looked obscene, and he'd love to see it. Maybe next time, they could swap places.

"Like what you see?" he gasped.

Heath licked his lips and nodded. "You stretch beautifully for my cock."

Rory's hips stuttered. He dragged himself forward and was wrenched back, over and over, the push and pull, lighting his channel. "Fuck, Heath. Yeah, take me."

The room filled with harsh breathing and the slap of skin on skin, interspersed with dirty words and curses while they reached for their climax.

"Come here," Heath gritted out, reaching under Rory's arms to lift him upright again. "Circle your hips. I'm close."

Rory laid his head back on Heath's shoulder, his hips moving. Heath plucked at Rory's nub while his other encircled his cock.

There was so much sensation flowing through Rory, he couldn't stem the orgasm that appeared from nowhere. He shouted his release, feeling his ass clench down on Heath's cock as his own spurted on his stomach and over Heath's hand. Heath grunted in his ear, the arm around his waist tightening as he came.

Rory didn't want to move, but he knew Heath had to dispose of the condom, so he reluctantly crawled forward, groaning at the sensitivity when Heath withdrew. His ass felt empty, and he dropped to the bed, eyes closed.

He felt himself being lifted and blinked open his eyes. Heath deposited him with his head on a pillow, laid next to him and pulled the covers over them. When they settled, Heath chuckled.

Rory frowned at him. "If I wasn't so exhausted, laughter following sex would offend me," he mumbled.

"Sorry. I was just thinking about what I came to tell you."

"Which was?" Rory peered over at him.

"I wanted to tell you I was sorry for holding back and to ask if we could go back to the way things were. I think I have my answer, though."

Rory smiled lazily and rested his head on Heath's chest. "I was fed up with the tiptoeing around we were doing. I had planned to seduce you, but I think we seduced each other."

"I am sorry. Again. I thought I was doing the right thing by giving you space, but I think I just made things worse." Heath ran his fingers up and down Rory's arm.

"No, we're both to blame. Let's just take it day by day, minute by minute, and see what happens."

"Agreed."

"I'm tired. Stay with me?"

"As long as you'll have me."

# 19

# Heath

"I don't think it's working, Rory!" he called.

Rory stopped running and headed back his way, his dark tattoos gleaming against his pale skin in the meagre sunlight. His polo shirt stuck to him like a second skin, and Heath licked his lips in remembrance of the way he'd tongued down those abs the previous night. The jeans Rory wore were loose, but there was no denying the strength in those legs, despite how slim they were.

"Seen enough?" The amused tone broke through his thoughts, and Heath smirked.

"Not nearly enou—"

"Heath! We need you!"

He turned at Emma's frantic voice, seeing her running towards him.

"What's wrong?"

"Flossie's not well," she panted.

"All right, stay and help me, Emma, while Heath goes to check on her." Rory's voice wavered but stayed strong when he nodded in Heath's direction.

Heath said nothing but turned and ran. When he got closer to the kennels, he saw Carlton standing outside Flossie's, holding the vet bag he always left in Rory's office when it wasn't being used.

"What happened?" he asked when he reached him and entered the kennel.

Carlton shook his head. "No idea. She was fine when we fed her breakfast this morning, and I just came into check on each of them, as I do, and she was like this. I haven't touched her or anything."

The tone Carlton used had Heath understanding what Carlton hadn't said. He knelt beside the black and white Border Collie and ran his hands over her. Right away, he knew Carlton was correct, but he went through his checks anyway, unable to leave things to chance. After he'd spent several minutes with her, Rory came in, standing with Carlton.

Heath hated to be the bearer of bad news, but there was no getting away from it. He glanced up at Rory, and Rory's nostrils flared as he closed his eyes, knowing what Heath hadn't vocalised.

"Carlton? Can you see that she's comfortably wrapped in a blanket, please? We can arrange things later today. I'm going to..." He pointed towards Rory and stood.

Carlton nodded and moved out of their way. Heath rested his hand on Rory's arm, trying not to startle him, then turned him towards the door, holding him steady with an arm around his waist. Heath led him to the main building and through to his office, sitting Rory in his chair. He plucked a blanket from a pile just outside the door and tucked it around Rory, kneeling in front of him.

Rory's blank gaze was terrifying but understandable. "Remember, Rory, she was getting on in years. She's had a long life, and she spent her last days surrounded by other dogs and people who cared about her."

"Maybe I'm not cut out for this job," Rory muttered, head lowering. "I'm sad when people adopt the dogs, but when they die...devastated doesn't even come close. I feel like a failure."

"You're not! You're giving these dogs a chance at a new or better life. Flossie was fourteen, Rory. She was above the average age for her breed. She's had a fantastic long life, especially because she had suffered no abuse. She came here because her elderly owner died, didn't she?" Rory nodded slowly. "There you go, then. Flossie looks like she was sleeping when it happened. Such a nice way to join her previous owner."

Heath wasn't sure if he believed in the afterlife, but he wanted to.

"Heath?" He turned and saw Emma at the door. "I brought coffee."

He stood, taking the mugs from her hands. "Are you okay?" he asked quietly.

She nodded. "Look after him. He always takes this harder than anyone else," she whispered.

"I will. Thanks for the drinks."

She closed the office door behind her, and Heath took the drinks over to the desk. He set them down, then grabbed a chair from the other side of the desk and dragged it in front of Rory. It was a tight fit with how small the office was and how much furniture was already in there, but he managed. When he sat with his knees bracketing Rory's legs, he gave the hot drink to Rory, making sure he had a good hold on it before letting it go. The last thing they needed was hot liquid burning either of them.

They sat in silence while they drank, neither of them needing to be anywhere else. Heath wasn't sure how long it had been when Rory finally put his mug back on the desk and shuffled forward onto Heath's lap. Heath had already put his drink down, so he wrapped his arms around Rory, and his boyfriend tucked his head into Heath's neck. He rubbed his hand up and down Rory's spine, feeling the tension slowly releasing.

"She was happy. Always glad to see us," Rory murmured.

"She was."

Rory sat upright. "All right." He blew out a breath. "I'm good. Let's sort things out for her."

"You sure?"

He nodded and gave a small smile. "Yeah. Maybe I'm too soft for this job. I hate it when dogs leave, no matter how they leave."

"No, that makes you human." Rory headed to the door. "I just have to make a couple of calls, and I'll be with you."

He watched while Rory left, then pulled out his phone. "Mum? Would it be possible for us to come for dinner tonight?" When she agreed, he briefly detailed what had happened so she wouldn't be expecting an enormous amount of conversation, but Heath believed being around family would help Rory deal with Flossie's passing.

After he'd hung up, he made a note to ask Rory if they buried the dogs. What they did would depend on who he needed to call next.

• • • ● ● • ● ● • • •

Rory hadn't been sure he'd be good enough company for Heath's parents, but Heath had compromised and said they could leave if he wasn't feeling it. When his mother pulled Rory into a hug after they entered, he saw Rory relax with whatever Grace said to him.

"Come on. Dinner's waiting." His mother led the way to the kitchen, and Heath threaded his fingers through Rory's.

"Are you okay?"

Rory turned damp eyes to him and smiled. "Yeah, I'm good. This was a great idea."

"Nothing beats the blues like my mum's cooking. Except maybe my jokes." Heath cocked his head, looking to the side as if thinking.

Rory snorted. "Don't give up your day job."

"That's what I used to tell him," Parker hollered when he came in behind them. "He always thought he was hot shit when it came to jokes." Parker shook his head. "He's never learned."

"I am hot shit. My jokes are legendary." Heath poked his nose in the air and took a seat to Rory's right.

Rory grinned. "Do you want to tell them the one you told me near the beginning of when we first met?"

Heath flushed. "Maybe not."

"Come on! You gotta tell us! We need all the evidence we can get." Parker sat across from them, a pleading look on his face, and he clasped his hands beneath his chin.

"He doesn't need to tell you anything. It's all good. I'm sure you have enough evidence, anyway." Heath stood from his chair and fetched the cutlery, setting them beside each placemat.

"That's true, but there's always room for more." Parker smirked.

"Now, now, children. Play nice." His dad entered the room, heading over to Grace and pecking her on the cheek. "Thank you, sweetheart," he whispered, although Heath just caught the words.

He loved it that his parents were still very much in love with each other and showed it in small ways. As he watched, his father took the large plate of meat from his mother's hands and carried it to the table. He was the kind of father and partner that Heath had always wished to be.

"Oh my god, he didn't?"

Heath switched his attention to Parker and Rory, seeing Rory's sheepish expression as opposed to Parker's gleeful one.

"You just told him, didn't you?" Heath rolled his eyes when Rory bit his lip and nodded.

"Priceless," Parker said.

Regardless of the teasing he knew would ensue with his jokes exposed, he was glad to see an easing of the sadness on Rory's face. He knew it would take time for the grief to become bearable, but with everyone around him helping, Rory would be fine. It wasn't just the pain of Flossie but also the anguish of losing his parents.

Heath would be there every step of the way.

# 20

# Rory

It had taken a few weeks before Rory felt like himself again. The same thing happened every time a dog passed away. Rory had been at the shelter for around nine months, and they had lost five dogs in that time. Each time, Rory felt it just as deeply as the previous one. One little dot of a thing that had helped, though, had been Spencer.

There had been no interest in adoption for the little dog. Rory had tried again since Flossie had died, trying to increase interest in the little pug, but no one wanted the gorgeous dog. A thought had been circling his mind, but he wasn't sure if it was the best thing for Spencer or not. He needed to talk to Heath about it, which he could do in a couple of hours.

He spent the afternoon on paperwork. It seemed to be his primary activity lately. Rory hadn't been joking when he'd said the paperwork multiplied. He was certain it did. How, he hadn't figured out yet, but he would.

A knock on the door brought his attention back, and he smiled when Heath entered and walked around the desk to press a kiss to Rory's lips. Rory whimpered when Heath pulled away, but Heath just chuckled.

"Nice to see you, too," Heath said.

Rory closed his eyes, sighed and smiled, some of the tension leaving his body in Heath's presence.

"You seem busy."

Rory snorted. "Aren't I always? Haven't you figured out how to neuter this paperwork yet?" he joked.

"It's on my to-do list."

"Can you bump it up the list?" Rory grinned. "Anyway, I wanted your opinion on something." He stood, rounding the desk. "Follow me."

"Anywhere."

Rory hid his smile behind his hand and headed for the kennels. Heath had been saying things like that ever since they'd figured out their relationship, and it made Rory's heart flutter each time. Their hands brushed while they walked side by side across the grass, the dogs barking their greetings as Rory and Heath came closer. Rory padded to Spencer's kennel and opened the door, kneeling when Spencer came waddling up to him for a fuss.

"Who's a good boy?" Rory sat on the cold floor, pulling Spencer onto his lap. Heath sat beside him, a slight crease between his eyes. "I've been thinking about his little guy and wanted to ask what you thought about my idea." Heath nodded. "What if I adopted him, and he could stay with me at the shelter when I'm working and sleep in the house at night? Do you think he would be okay doing that? Do you think he'd manage?"

Heath smiled. "I think he'd love that." He glanced down at the small dog nestled on Rory's lap, reaching forward to scratch at his rump. "As much as he loves it in the kennel, he would get so much from being around you. And if you want..." Heath hesitated.

"What?"

He rolled his lips inwards. "I could sometimes take him to the clinic with me, too. I'm sure the staff would love him just as much."

Rory beamed. "I bet they would, but only if you're sure."

"Having the little guy around would only add to what we have, Rory, never take away from it."

Rory leaned forward and pressed a kiss to Heath's lips. "Thank you."

"Rory, sorry. Someone is asking about the owner," Angie said.

"I'll be right there, Angie." Rory glanced down at Spencer. "I'll be back later, buddy." He heard a disgruntled noise from the dog when Rory moved him to his bed, and he chuckled. "You can snuggle later."

"Me, too. I hope," Heath said.

"Of course." Rory pecked him on the lips. "Head over to the house. I'll be over as soon as I'm done."

He strode towards the main building, his heart bursting with love for the two men in his life. Hopefully, soon, he can persuade Heath to make their living situation permanent.

Entering the front reception, Rory greeted the man. "How can I help you?"

"I'm interested in buying this place," the man said, his voice soft but precise as if English was his second language.

Rory frowned. "As far as I'm aware, the owner is not looking to sell, but I can ask him to call you."

"Would you mind calling him now and seeing if he will talk? I'm really interested and have ideas about how to expand."

Rory's eyes widened. "I-I can try him. Just give me a moment." He left the guy in reception with Angie and headed to his office, shutting the door behind him. He wasn't sure how to explain to Mr Harding about what the guy wanted but dialled his number, anyway.

"Mr Stephenson, what can I do for you?" The harsh tone was the natural voice for the owner.

"Mr Harding, I'm sorry to bother you. I have a gentleman here who wants to buy the shelter. I'm not really sure what you want me to do?"

Mr Harding was quiet for a moment. "Is he still there?"

"Yes."

"Take the phone to him."

Rory rolled his eyes at the order, wishing he could remind the guy to use his manners, but he refrained...just. He muted the phone and headed back to reception. "I have Mr Harding on the phone." He unmuted the line and held it out.

"Mr Harding? Yes, I'm Niklaus Kalchik. I would like to buy the shelter."

Rory watched the man paced around the area, talking and listening. Rory couldn't hear both sides of the conversation, but there didn't seem to be any animosity in the guy's demeanour.

"That's great news, Mr Harding. I'll be in touch."

Rory's eyebrows rose when Mr Kalchik handed him his phone. "Everything okay?"

The man grinned, the expression softening his features. "Everything's perfect. Mr Harding has agreed. As soon as we have finalised the terms, the shelter will be transferred to my ownership."

"Mr Kalchik, can I ask...why are you interested in buying this place?"

The man leaned his elbows on the counter. "Klaus, please. I've recently moved to the area, and I love dogs. I would love to be part of something so vital to the community, and with the money I can invest, we can do wonders with the place."

Rory's heart raced. If this was true, then things were looking up. "Will all the staff still have their jobs?"

"Definitely. I will not be firing anyone. If anything, I will bring more people on."

"That's..." Rory shook his head. "That's great. Do you want to have a look around?"

"Not toda—"

"Rory? I've locked everything—"

Rory glanced at Carlton to see his eyes wide, his mouth open, and his movements frozen. He switched his attention to Klaus, who appeared to have softened further and had a small smile on his face.

"Do you two..." he started.

"Klaus. What are you doing here?" Carlton asked, jaw clenching.

"Carl. I've just moved to Cambridge," Klaus answered quietly.

Rory raised his eyebrows, and the tension mounted. "Klaus is buying the shelter."

Carlton frowned, then swallowed and turned his attention to Rory. "I've locked everything up out back, so there's just the front to do when you're ready. I'm going to head out if that's okay?"

"Sure. Thanks, Carlton."

Carlton glanced in Klaus's direction once more before heading back the way he came. Rory stared at Klaus. "Is that going to be a problem?"

Klaus shook his head and curled the corner of his mouth. "Nothing I can't handle."

"Nice to meet you, Klaus."

"You, too, Rory. Angie."

Rory watched Klaus leave the main building, the man's attention on the fence separating the car park from the kennels. "Well, that was interesting," he murmured.

# 21

# Heath

He'd just taken Dexter for a walk around the field. He was a lively little terrier, and he was mischievous as hell. Case in point, when he slipped his lead and scurried towards the main building instead of to his kennel where his food was waiting.

Heath dashed through the maze, keeping his eye on where Dexter was going. "Dexter! Get back here. You're going the wrong way if you want food, dog," he grumbled, hearing the front door open.

He grabbed the playful pup when he entered reception. Luckily, the people were still on the other side of the gate, so Dexter couldn't escape. He lifted his gaze. "Welcome to…" He paused when he focused on the visitors and recognised Casey, Marcus's ex. He saw the guy reach out for another man who stood next to him, hands clasping. Heath understood the reason and wanted to reassure Casey.

"He's an asshole, and I've not spoken to him for months. You have nothing to worry about from me. I promise." Heath stayed still, hoping the words would sink in.

The guy Casey had moved closer to glanced between them, then said, "Who are you?"

"I'm Heath. I *was* friends with Marcus."

The guy turned his attention to Casey and, when Casey looked at him, asked, "Do you want to stay?"

Casey focused on Heath again, then nodded.

Heath relaxed a little and smiled. "Come on through. Please lock the gate behind you. I'm going to grab Rory."

Heath left the three men in the foyer and hustled to Rory's office. "Hey, Rory? We have some visitors." He cleared his throat. "It's Marcus's ex and two others. I think he's a little skittish about me, so I'm going to make myself scarce if that's okay?"

Rory rounded the desk and stopped in front of him, scratching between Dexter's ears while he studied Heath. "Are you all right?"

"Yes. I just feel awful for how Marcus treated him, and as far as Casey knew, we were still close friends. I've told him we're not now, but I don't know if he believes me."

"Don't worry. I'll deal with them. Go put Dexter back, then head over to the house if you want."

"Nah, I'll go help Carlton in the storage shed."

"Okay. I think Emma's in there with him, so send her out when you get there, please."

"Will do." Heath leaned forward and pressed their lips together before Rory left. He stayed where he was for a moment, listening to Rory's greeting.

"Hi. Welcome to All Seasons Animal Shelter. I'm the manager, Rory. What pet can I get you today? Oh, sorry, we only have dogs!"

The laughter that followed made Heath smile, and he headed to the kennels. He saw peeks of Casey and the other men walking the dogs over the next hour, and it was only when he saw them head back towards the main building that he headed the same way. He wasn't planning on approaching them again, but he wanted to hear Casey sounding normal instead of... almost frightened.

When Rory came around the corner, Heath made a split-second decision. "I've just got to..." He didn't finish as he jogged towards the entrance.

"Casey!" he called across the car park.

He didn't get too close, but close enough, he didn't have to shout. The guy with whom Casey appeared to be in a relationship wrapped his arm around Casey's shoulders.

"I am sorry about Marcus. I never believed he was like that. I've known him for over five years, and he's never shown any kind of behaviour that had me concerned." He sighed. "As soon as I heard about it, I spoke to Marcus. He confirmed everything and didn't seem repentant, so I told him to stay away from me. I've not seen him since."

"I'm sorry you lost your friend," Casey said, his voice shaking.

"I'm sorry he hurt you."

Casey thumbed behind him. "We have to go."

Heath nodded and retreated to the shelter. There was nothing more he could do. When he entered, Rory came to him, holding him tight.

"You did all you could."

"I know. I still feel bad, though."

Rory pulled back, cupping Heath's jaw. "It's in your nature." He smiled. "Come on, we have four dogs who have just been adopted, which means...?"

Heath groaned. "More paperwork."

"Yay! More paperwork." Rory blew out a breath. "At least this paperwork is the good kind."

"When is Klaus getting here?"

Rory checked his watch. "In about an hour, I believe. Around the same time as Mr Harding and his lawyers."

"I can't believe you're going to be out from under that idiot's reign of terror." Heath cheered.

"It wasn't so bad, but from the dealings I've had with Klaus so far, he seems a lot better. The best thing is that he's willing to spend money and not just make it."

"Yes. That should make things less stressful for you."

Rory turned to him when they entered his office. "But you enjoy helping me relieve stress..." He draped his arms around Heath's neck, nuzzling under his ear.

Heath held Rory's hips, closed his eyes and tilted his head. "I do. Just not here." He pushed Rory away. "Remember when Angie caught us last time?"

Rory howled. "She should've knocked."

"Well, she won't ever not knock again, will she?" Heath glanced down when something nudged his shin. "Hey, you. You've been a sleepyhead today." He crouched down to pick up Spencer and held him tight.

"Oh, so he can have cuddles, but I can't. Is that how things are?"

"Definitely." Heath pivoted away.

"Spencer, you traitor!" Rory called after them, making Heath chuckle.

He headed for the kennels. The shelter recently had an abused pug come in, and the little guy was very skittish. They'd tried putting Spencer in with the new dog, who they'd named Leo, and it had worked wonders. So, every day, Spencer spent a bit of his day with his new playmate, and if Heath was a betting man, he was sure Rory would soon have a new dog. Or maybe Heath would.

Or if Heath had his way, maybe they both would.

After he introduced the two dogs again, he closed the door behind him and set off to do whatever work needed to be done before the two owners—new and old—arrived.

They were still no closer to a revelation about how Carlton and Klaus knew each other. Carlton avoided any questions that cropped up about it, changing the subject every time. He couldn't avoid the man himself because he was going to be the owner, and as such, had visited several times to get the lay of the land.

Klaus had spent some time with each of the employees, except Carlton. Heath believed it was for two reasons: one, they already knew each other, and two, Carlton tried to avoid being in the same room as the guy.

Both he and Rory believed there was a shared history between them, maybe even a relationship, but they wouldn't pry more than they had already tried to do.

The process took less time than anyone expected, even Klaus, and when the day drew to a close, there was excitement in the air when the transfer of ownership had been signed, and Mr Harding left without a goodbye for anyone. Klaus, on the other hand, stayed to celebrate, bringing some beer in from his car that he'd kept in a chiller box.

"I know you are still on the clock, but as the new owner, I will allow this one drink to our success. Cheers."

"Cheers!"

Heath slipped his arm around Rory's waist. "I think things are looking up."

Rory stared at him. "I hope so."

# 22

# Rory

Rory was scared. He hoped they would have a second event to celebrate when he and Heath headed back to Rory's house, but he honestly had no idea what Heath was going to say. He wanted to get it over and done with so, either way, he would have an answer, but everyone was intent on celebrating the new owner.

Rory had to agree that Klaus seemed like a genuinely pleasant person. When he'd approached Carlton about the guy, all Carlton had said was that if Klaus had promised something, he would deliver, which reduced Rory's stress but made him worry even more about Carlton and Klaus's past. It was none of his business, though, but he made sure Carlton knew he could come to him if he needed anything.

When things finally settled down, the staff completed the day's work and locked everything up. After saying goodnight to everyone and locking the front door behind them, Rory and Heath headed through the main building, switching off lights as they went, then headed to the kennels to pick up Spencer. They found the two pugs snuggled up together on the bed, so left them together for the night. It wasn't the first time it had happened, and he doubted it would be the last. They were both so cute.

They walked, hand in hand, to the house, the outdoor lights leading the way. Rory's hand shook when he unlocked the house and held the door open for Heath to follow. He had plans, but he didn't know whether to get it over and done with now or later.

"What's the matter?" Rory jumped. "Exactly my point. Why are you scared?"

Heath was far too observant.

"I...Well, I wanted...to ask you something."

"If it's to do with the dogs, I think I know what you're going to ask."

Rory frowned. "The dogs?"

"Yeah, Spencer and Leo. I've seen how you look at them." Heath grinned. "If you want to adopt Leo, it's fine by me."

Rory dropped his head and smiled. "Thanks." He exhaled. "But it's not about them. Although that is good to know."

"What is it, then?"

"Well, you know how you're always here, helping when you're not at the clinic. Or when you stay over, which I love, by the way...What if..." Rory took a breath, trying to settle his nerves. "What if you stayed here? All the time. Instead of having your house and my house, we can join them. Not physically join the houses, of course. But we could ha—"

Heath's mouth suddenly occupied Rory's, holding him still so he could kiss him. Rory mewled when Heath pulled away.

"I'd love to move in. Or you could move to mine, whichever you'd prefer."

"Really?"

"Yes, now kiss me."

He did. Their lips met, and his heart raced, knowing they had taken the next step in healing the small crack that had appeared when Rory's parents had tried to split them up. When they broke for air, Rory grabbed Heath's hand and turned to the stairs, climbing as fast as he could while keeping a tight hold of him.

In his room, Rory stopped at the end of his bed and faced the man who meant so much to him.

"Will you fuck me, Rory?" Heath breathed into his ear. "I want to feel you inside me."

Rory tilted his head, and Heath nuzzled his neck. "Yes. Oh god, yes." He pulled away, peeling off his T-shirt and toeing off his shoes at the same time.

Heath chuckled, then followed suit, yanking his clothes off and throwing them to the side. When both were naked, they collided, mouths devouring, hands groping, hips thrusting until they fell to the bed, Heath underneath him.

Rory kissed his way down Heath's chest, fingers playing with his nipples as Rory's mouth moved closer to his goal. With Heath's stiff cock in front of him, Rory paused, taking in the sight of the dark pink flesh. He ran his nose up the underside of it, inhaling Heath's scent while he went, then, reaching the head, flicked his tongue over it to taste him.

Heath groaned, and his fingers raked through Rory's hair while Rory's taste buds savoured every inch. When he'd had enough—at least for the moment—Rory sat upright. "Roll over." Heath did, spreading his legs, and Rory proceeded to lick and bite at Heath's ass until there were red marks all over his cheeks. "Mine." He hadn't meant to growl it, but the idea that Heath would move onto someone else made him want to stake a claim.

"Yes," Heath murmured.

Rory snatched the supplies from the drawer and settled back on his knees. Popping the lid of the lube, he squirted some onto his fingers and spread Heath's cheeks, licking his lips at the sight. Pressing his finger against the rosebud, he circled a few times before Heath relaxed enough for Rory to push through. Heath's groan of pleasure was heard but also felt through the tightening of his muscles. Rory took his time, sliding his finger in and out, watching it disappear into Heath and reappear slick. When

Heath was pushing back, Rory added another finger, rotating his hand and scissoring his fingers to stretch him further, making sure the sounds coming from Heath were pleasurable ones, not pain-filled.

Adding a third finger was nearly Rory's undoing. "You look decadent like this, Heath. All spread out, taking my fingers and wanting more." He didn't know where the talk was coming from; he had never been like this with anyone else.

"Please, Rory."

"A little more." Heath probably was more than ready, but Rory didn't want to stop what he was doing just yet.

"Rory! Please!"

Rory took his attention from his fingers and saw Heath gripping the sheets by his head, his teeth biting into the pillow, and he caved. Pulling his fingers free with a protest from below, Rory rolled on the condom and slicked it up. Bracing himself on one hand, he guided his cock to Heath's entrance, breaching the ring of muscles before sliding deep. When he was as close as he could get, he paused, breathing hard.

"Move, please!"

"Patience, Heath." Rory's chuckle turned into a moan when the movement vibrated through him. Holding himself off Heath, he lifted each of his legs over Heath's, pushing Heath's legs together until Rory was straddling him, his cock still deep inside the willing hole. "Tell me if this is uncomfortable at any point."

"Uh-huh."

Rory withdrew a little, then thrust forward, repeating the action several times to make sure Heath was all right with the motion. Once he received several pleasure-filled sounds, he slid in and lowered himself to Heath's back, blanketing him. Threading their fingers by the pillow, Rory made small movements with his hips, and he kissed and licked whatever skin he could reach.

He could feel the sweat gathering between them as his hips increased, his backside clenching on the inward slide to shove his cock harder into Heath.

"Fuck, Heath. Can you hear that? The wet glide of my cock burying itself inside your sweet ass. The sounds alone could make me come." He thrust faster, his pulse increasing as well.

"God! Harder, please! Please, Rory!" The grip of Heath's fingers on him was painful but not as painful as it would be if he stopped what he was doing.

Rory felt himself getting closer and knew they needed more. He paused, and Heath whimpered his displeasure. Unlinking their fingers, Rory pushed to his hands, keeping his cock buried, he slid his legs between Heath's, spreading his lover out in front of him. Rory transferred his grip to Heath's hips and held him tight so Rory didn't slip out. The change in position had Rory rooting in further, if that was possible.

Once he was kneeling, Rory took a breath, sweat beading on his skin and dripping down his chest.

"You ready for more?" Rory asked.

Heath's eyes blinked open, finding Rory, then nodded. "Make me come, Rory."

"My pleasure."

Gripping Heath's hips, Rory used it as leverage while he withdrew slowly, then plunged forward, deeper than before.

"Oh, holy fuck!" Heath turned his face into the pillow, his hand reaching for his dick while Rory pounded his ass.

The position had Rory as deep as he could go. "Fucking hell, Heath. Your ass is gold. Fucking tight and hot." He pistoned his hips, gripping Heath's leg and ass hard. "I'm gonna come. Come with me, Heath. Come on, baby. Fuck!"

"Oh, god! Oh, fuck, ah!"

Rory felt it when Heath released, his channel clenching tighter around his cock. Rory's brain misfired, and he came with a growl.

When he couldn't stay upright any longer, he pulled out and rolled onto his back, panting when he removed and tied off the condom.

"Jesus, Heath. I feel like I've run a marathon."

Unintelligible noises came from Heath's direction, and Rory huffed a breath. When he regained some energy, he stumbled to the bathroom, disposing of the condom and wetting a flannel. Heath was still in the same position when he returned, so he carefully wiped him down and threw the flannel in the direction of the washing basket.

Pulling the covers over them, he spooned behind Heath and kissed his neck, knowing there was nowhere else he'd rather be.

# 23

# Heath

"Is there any furniture you need?" he asked Rory one evening. "I have a house full, but you don't have to have any of it."

"This is your house as well now, Heath. The question should be if there is any furniture you would like to bring?"

Rory placed the box on the table with the other ones, then turned to face him.

"Maybe my desk if we can find room for it."

Rory came to stand in front of him, draping his arms around his neck, and pressed a kiss to his lips. "Well, before you decide to leave everything, I have some news."

Heath raised his eyebrows. "I'm all ears."

"Klaus informed me the other day about his plans for the new buildings he's setting up."

Heath nodded, not understanding where Rory was going with this information. "Okay. What's that got to do with me living here?"

"Well, he asked me if I'd like to have the house extended a little."

"Seriously? I didn't think he'd be bothered about that."

"Me, either."

"What did you tell him?"

"That we would love to have a slightly bigger place."

Heath grinned. "I can't believe he agreed to it."

"I wasn't expecting it. He's certainly sinking some money into this place."

Heath nuzzled into Rory's neck. "I think it might have something to do with a certain employee."

"Hmm." Rory tilted his head, allowing Heath access to his exposed skin, which he happily took advantage of.

After a few seconds, Rory pulled away. "No! We're supposed to be going to your parents' for dinner. If we start this, we'll be late." He held his palm up when Heath tried to get close again.

He pouted. "Spoilsport."

"Turn those puppy dog eyes on someone else, Mister. I'm immune."

"Do you want to test that theory?"

Rory hesitated but shook his head and chuckled. "Not today." Heath smacked Rory's ass when he turned away, and Rory yelped and jumped. "Heath!"

Heath grinned. "Sorry, couldn't help myself."

"Well, try to." Heath could tell Rory tried to look stern, but he just couldn't do it.

He caught him in his arms again, moulding himself to Rory's back and wrapped him tight against him. Rory rested his head on Heath's shoulder, and Heath tucked his face into Rory's neck—his favourite place. "I love you, Rory," he whispered.

Rory pressed a kiss to his temple. "I love you, too."

They stayed plastered together for a few minutes, luxuriating in the peace they'd found with each other.

"Are we taking the dogs with us?"

"I think we better. It annoyed Mum when we didn't take them last time, if you remember."

Rory chuckled. "Yeah. I didn't think they'd take to them so quickly."

"Me, either. You never know; they might end up visiting to find one for themselves."

Rory spun around, and Heath let him go. "Ooh, I know the perfect one for them! Sophie! She'd be perfect." Rory bit his lip. "Do you think…"

"No. Rory, no." He knew what his boyfriend was thinking.

"But why not? If we take her with us, too, they might not want her to leave." Rory smiled, jubilant with his idea.

Heath wasn't so sure, but as usual, he couldn't help but let Rory get his way, even though he disagreed. At the end of the day, if his parents didn't like the dog, they'd bring her back to the shelter.

After they had secured the three dogs in the car, Heath drove them across the city. Even though he didn't think it would work, he was excited to see his mum's reaction to the dog. They'd owned a family dog when Heath was younger, but Pippa had passed away before he'd reached his teenage years, and they had never replaced her.

When they arrived, Heath took Spencer's and Leo's leads, and he left Rory with Sophie. At Rory's uneasy look, Heath grinned. "It was your idea."

"Thanks," Rory deadpanned.

They entered the house, calling out a greeting and trooped into the living room.

"Have you brought those dogs this time?" his mother called from the kitchen.

"Yes, Mum!" he replied.

"Oh, let me see." She came bustling into the room, dropping straight into her armchair, so she could fuss over the little devils. "Oh, aren't they the sweetest? And so well behaved." Her gaze flicked to Sophie. "You never told me you'd adopted another one. Come over here, beautiful. What's her name?"

"Sophie. And we haven't adopted her. We just thought…" Rory looked over at him, a helpless expression on his face.

"*You* just thought. Don't bring me into this."

Rory narrowed his gaze, indicating Heath would be in trouble later. "I wondered if she was a dog you might be interested in."

"Oh." Grace stroked Sophie's coat, and Sophie did her part and sat nicely, allowing his mother to pet her. "She's very calm." Sophie dropped her chin to his mother's knee, and Heath hid a smile. Sophie knew what she was doing. "Oh. Bill?" Grace looked over at his father, who smiled at his wife. "What do you think?"

"It's up to you, sweetheart. I'd be more than happy to have her keep us company."

Grace returned her attention to Sophie and smiled. "Well, Sophie. I guess we're going to say welcome to the family." She narrowed her eyes at Rory. "As for you," she pointed a finger at him, "no more bringing any dogs here that aren't already part of the family. We definitely can't have more than one living here."

Rory ducked his head. "Yes, Grace. I'm sorry."

"Don't be sorry, dear boy. You brought this beautiful girl into our lives. Just don't do it again."

Heath chuckled. "No guarantees, Mum. He's a force of nature."

"We'll need to get some supplies for her."

"I can do that after dinner if you'd like me to," Rory offered. "It's the least I can do."

"Thank you, dear." Grace gave the dogs one more fuss each, then stood. "Right, dinner is almost ready. Come and set the table, boys. Bill, can you sort the drinks?"

"Of course." Bill stood, folding his paper and placing it on the table.

His mother had brought them up to help out in the house, regardless of the gender-specific jobs that were prevalent in the world. According to her, and rightly so, if she did all the "women's" jobs, she'd be working twenty-four hours a day, and she wasn't having that. Therefore, as soon as they were old enough, they had chores to do, swapping around regularly, ensuring they weren't always doing the jobs they hated.

Heath thought it was a fair exchange, especially since their mother cooked every day. Luckily, it was something she enjoyed, so never minded doing it. Although it hadn't stopped her from teaching the kids to cook. Far from it. Every week, they would have two lessons each on how to cook certain meals, meaning Heath's ability was beyond some men his age, and he was immensely grateful for it.

They settled the dogs in the hallway, so they wouldn't be begging for food, and then sat to swap stories about their week, which had been their routine for the past few weeks. Heath and Rory explained about the potential house extension and asked about Parker, who had been absent more than present at the meals lately. His mother told them about his new girlfriend and that she hadn't met her yet. Her feelings on that subject were more than clear without her having to say a word.

Looking around the table, Heath was more content than ever.

# 24

# Rory

Rory wished Carlton and Klaus would sort things out between them, whatever it was. Although there were no arguments at the shelter, he could cut the tension with a knife every time they were in the vicinity of each other.

He was still none the wiser as to the reason for their behaviour, and it wasn't really his place to ask. If it carried on too much longer, though, he would bring it up with both of them. Not at the same time, which was sure to cause a rift, but individually, he might understand the dissension.

Apart from that, life was great. The improvements made to the shelter were already bringing in more revenue and customers, but also more dogs. With the kennels extended and several more added on, they could house more of them. Rory loved that because he hated turning dogs in need away when he had no room. He was sure that would still happen in the future, but at least he had a bit of a reprieve while some kennels were still empty.

As for the main building, it was undergoing a renovation, too. Walls were being knocked down to make the rooms larger, including his office, which had overjoyed Rory. It had been the first job Klaus had insisted upon when he'd seen the cramped room where Rory spent most his time. Now, it was the size of two rooms and had two desks, several filing cabinets, three sets of shelving and a coffee machine—just for him. He'd almost hugged the owner when he'd seen that.

Despite the noise of the renovations, the extra space had made his work life much better, and with help from Emma, whom he'd found out was getting a business degree alongside the veterinarian one, he'd been able to figure out a better way to slimline the paperwork side of things.

"Are you almost done?"

Carlton's voice broke into his thoughts.

"Hey. I probably have another half an hour, and I'll leave it at that for the day."

"Glad to see you're only working the hours you should be now, instead of all the hours under the sun."

"Yeah, it's nice to finish at a reasonable hour and not have palpitations because the paper pile didn't seem any smaller." He chuckled.

"I'm heading to a bar tomorrow night. I wasn't sure if you and Heath wanted to join me?"

Rory raised his eyebrows. It was the first social event, outside of the work that they would go on if they accepted. "Let me check with Heath, but I don't see it being a problem."

They agreed on the details, and Carlton waved goodbye. It would be nice to get to know who Carlton was away from work. Rory still didn't have many friends, but he'd decided several weeks ago that he needed people around him he liked and trusted, and if he couldn't find those people, then it was their loss, not his.

He concentrated on his work, then closed down the computer and checked to make sure everything was locked and switched off. While he wandered through the shelter towards home, he thought of how much his life had changed within the last year. He never would've believed how different things would be if someone had told him before.

Rory unlocked the front door, the scent of cooked food teasing his nostrils when he entered. "Hmm. Something smells nice." Locking the door behind him, he slipped off his shoes and peeked his head around the corner of the kitchen. He gasped when he saw he had set the table with a white tablecloth, two long-stemmed candles burning brightly, and a small vase of flowers to one side. "What is all this for?"

Heath glanced over his shoulder with a smile. "Do I have to have a reason other than I love you?"

"No, but..." He blew out a breath. "This looks amazing. Thank you."

"You're welcome." Heath dried his hands on a towel that was hanging from his shoulder, then moved closer, holding Rory's hips and dipping his mouth for a kiss. After a brief caress, Heath continued, "You have time for a shower if you want one."

Rory grinned. "Are you saying I stink?"

"Nope. Not saying a word."

Rory shook his head and heard the underlying silent words. *Yes, you do.* "I'll have you know the dog smell is currently very fashionable. You'd do well to follow my lead."

Heath snorted. "Did you seriously just make a dog joke using the word 'lead?'"

Rory pulled away with a smirk. "I don't know what you mean." He turned and headed for the stairs, unable to remove the smile from his face.

Living with Heath had been the best decision they'd made. Whoever reached home first was the one to cook, at least during the week. Every Sunday, they went to Heath's parents for dinner. Sometimes Parker was there, sometimes not. Things appeared to be going well with his girlfriend, although Grace complained bitterly that he had not brought her around for a visit yet.

It felt as though Rory was part of their family now, which was a great feeling, especially because he'd heard nothing from his parents or Aggie since the events at the beginning of the year. He wasn't upset about it most of the time, but there was the odd moment when he wished things had been different and he was still in touch with them. Remembering their behaviour, though, soon put things back into perspective. He assumed Aggie felt the same way as his parents because he'd not heard a word from her.

He pushed everything to the back of his mind and switched on the shower. Heath had created a wonderful atmosphere, and Rory would not ruin it with thoughts of his family.

Scrubbing himself until he was sure he was sweet-smelling once more, he dried off and dressed in jeans and a shirt. He jogged down the stairs and found Heath plating the food.

"Just in time," Heath said. "Have a seat."

"Let me help."

"No, I've got it."

Rory smiled and sat, watching Heath bustle around the room before he brought over the plates. Rory inhaled when Heath put it in front of him, and his mouth watered at the sight of lemon, yellowfin sole, homemade chips and mushy peas. It might not have seemed like an exciting dish, but it was one of Rory's favourites, and Heath knew it.

Rory's stomach rumbled, making them both laugh.

"Tuck in before your stomach starts eating you."

They filled the time with conversation about the different aspects of their lives and catching up on what the other person had done. When their wine and food had disappeared, Heath steepled his hands in front of his mouth, and knowing Heath as he did, Rory tensed for bad news.

"What's wrong?"

Heath rubbed a hand over his mouth. "I have something for you, but I don't know how you're going to take it."

Rory frowned. He was about to ask what he was talking about when there was a knock at the door. "Fuck! I must've forgotten to lock the gate." He stood, panicking, but Heath was suddenly in front of him, hands on his shoulders.

"Calm down. It's fine. It's for you."

Rory blew out a breath. "What?" He was so confused.

"Come. Let's answer the door."

Heath led the way to the hallway, then he let go of Rory's hand and unlocked the door. When he pulled it open, Rory gaped.

There stood a woman who looked like she was about ready to pop a child out while carrying a car seat with another child in it. A woman he didn't think he'd ever see again. A woman who looked much older than she had the last time Rory had seen her.

"Aggie?"

Heath gently took the car seat from her, careful not to wake the sleeping child as he placed the seat on the floor. When Aggie stepped into the house, Rory could do no more than pull her into his arms, tears streaming down his cheeks.

"I don't understand," he whispered.

Aggie was crying into his shoulder, so he looked at Heath for an explanation.

"She called a few days ago. It was when you'd left your phone here. You know, when you had to run to the shelter for something." When Rory nodded, he continued, "I didn't want the call to be missed, so I answered. Aggie told me what was happening and what she was planning. So, I helped her. I hadn't planned on keeping it a secret, but Aggie was worried you wouldn't want her here."

Rory pushed Aggie out of his arms. "Aggie! Of course, I want you here." He shook his head. "What's been going on?"

"I hate my life, Rory. I can't do it anymore. I've tried to be strong and go through the motions, but I don't love my husband, and Mum and Dad...well, you know how they are. I didn't want Heath to warn you in case you turned me away. I thought it was less likely you would if I was here in person."

"Oh, Aggie. The only way I'd turn you away was if you were like Mum and Dad."

"No! I'm not. I promise."

Rory pulled her into a hug again, then released her. "Did you drive down?"

She nodded. "It was the only way. I left with the few things I had in the car and the clothes on my back."

"God, you must be exhausted." He looked at her. "How long have you got left?" He indicated her protruding stomach.

She rubbed a pale hand over it. "Three weeks. It's a girl. I'm calling her Drew."

Rory smiled and glanced at the car seat. "And who's this?"

She grinned. "That's Brody. He's just turned one."

Rory raised his eyebrows. "Well, you've got your hands full. Good job you have help in the guise of two uncles and two grandparents who will love them." With the last words, he glanced at Heath, seeing him nod and smile.

"Thank you, Rory." She looked at Heath. "And you. I appreciate all you did."

At Rory's questioning glance, Heath's cheeks coloured. "I just gave her some money for petrol and an ear when she needed it. She's going to be staying at my house for now."

His heart overflowed with love for the man standing there as if it meant nothing to do all this for Rory's sister. Getting his emotions under control, he said, "Well, tonight you can stay here, and then tomorrow, we will sort everything out."

After he settled Aggie and the baby into the spare room, which they had finally sorted out, luckily, he descended the stairs, finding Heath tidying the kitchen. He went over and wrapped himself around his boyfriend. Heath turned in his arms and held him tight.

"I'm sorry I didn't tell you."

Rory stared up at him. "It doesn't matter. I love you. So much. Thank you for what you did."

"I love you, too."

He knew this would be a trying time for them all. Although Aggie was out of their reach, his parents wouldn't let her go without a fight. Rory was ready to fight for them all.

No one would touch his family. Never again.

In the meantime, he would enjoy every minute of the day surrounded by the people who meant so much to him.

# 25

# Heath

The clinic had been doing well over the last ten months, and Heath had taken on another vet so he could work at both the clinic and the shelter. It also helped with the growing need for appointments because Donald had finally given in to his wife's nagging and retired completely—with the caveat that he could be on call should anyone need him. He wasn't such a grumpy old man as Heath had first thought; he just acted that way. Donald loved the animals, though; it was plain to see whenever he was with them.

Heath loved the shelter just as much as Rory did, and with Klaus now in charge, things had certainly perked up around the place. There was still the underlying tension between Klaus and Carlton, but it had lowered to a simmer now. If Heath wasn't mistaken, they were in the process of mending whatever bridges had been broken before.

"And what do you think, little man?" Heath asked the toddler, who was babbling and dribbling all over the pushchair. Heath had taken Brody with him on a walk with the dogs, giving Aggie a break so she could sleep while her nine-month-old baby also slept. He loved both kids, and he often wondered whether it was something he would like for himself and Rory in the future. It was something he needed to speak to Rory about.

He pushed Brody back towards the kennels, marvelling at the sight of the extensive renovations that had been done. Klaus had not been kidding when he'd said he was going to sink some money into the place. They had doubled the number of kennels, added three more storage sheds, extended the main building and extended Rory and Heath's house to make it into a four-bedroom, spacious home.

After he had stopped by each dog's temporary home, he unlocked Leo and Spencer's kennel and let the dogs trail behind them into the main building, where he knew Rory was working on paperwork.

"Hey, handsome!"

Rory bent down to kiss Brody on the head, chuckling when the toddler lifted a dribble-coated hand towards him. He reached for a tissue and wiped his hands before allowing Brody to touch him.

"What about me?" Heath pouted when Rory stood upright once more.

"Aww, you know you're handsome. You don't need me to tell you." Rory smiled, then leaned forward, pressing a kiss to Heath's lips. "How are you, gorgeous?"

Heath grinned, wrapping his arm around Rory's waist and stealing another kiss. "I'm good. Walter, Bess, Hannover and Sally have all had their exercise. I need to get to the clinic. I'll drop Brody back with Aggie before I go."

"Are you sure?"

Heath nodded. "Yeah, it's on my way."

"What would you like for dinner tonight?"

"I don't mind. Whatever. Or we could get takeaway if you don't want to cook." The routine they had of the person who arrived home first did the cooking was working well, and Rory knew that

Heath would have a late evening at the clinic that day. It would be eight o'clock before he was home.

"Hmm, Indian sounds good. What do you think?"

Heath dipped his head for another kiss before agreeing. "Perfect." He pulled back reluctantly, not wanting to leave but needing to. "I'll see you later. Love you."

"Love you. Bye, Brody." Rory ruffled the little boy's short curls.

Brody waved his arms in the air in excitement while Heath aimed the pushchair at the exit. It didn't take long to buckle the little guy into the car seat, and before he knew it. Heath was already at Aggie's house—well, his house, but Aggie rented it—though it was enough time for Brody to fall asleep. He carefully lifted Brody out of his seat and folded him against his chest. Knocking on Aggie's door, he hoped she had caught up with some sleep.

"Hey," she whispered, looking more awake than she had when he'd picked Brody up earlier that day.

"He fell asleep in the car." Heath stepped over the threshold and wandered to the front room, where Aggie had placed a travel cot for times like these. Manoeuvring Brody, he settled him down without waking him, much to his relief.

"Thank you," Aggie said, a hand on her chest. "I needed that sleep."

"I bet you did. Just remember to call if you need some more. We don't mind looking after the two of them overnight if you want to get a full night."

Aggie grinned. "If I did that, I would know what I was missing and would never get over the loss. At the moment, a full night of sleep is a distant memory."

Heath laughed. "Right, I have to get to work. We'll catch up this weekend at Mum's, okay?"

"Yes. We'll be there."

Heath's mother had opened her arms to Aggie and her kids as soon as she walked through the front door. Since then, Aggie had more than enough people to ask to babysit, but she was as stubborn as Rory could be and refused to entertain the idea unless she was so exhausted, she had no choice. Sometimes, one of them would just descend on her and take the kids for a few hours. She always argued, but he knew she was happy they loved the kids for who they were, rather than being loved for what they could achieve, like what would happen with Rory and Aggie's parents.

Luckily, they hadn't heard from them since the initial phone calls when Aggie's disappearance was first noticed.

Entering the clinic, he surveyed the clients, waving at a couple, then headed to the reception desk to notify Elaine he was there.

"Good afternoon, Elaine. How're things?"

"Flowing along nicely for a change. Although now that I've said that, I've jinxed it, haven't I?" She rolled her eyes and transferred her gaze to the computer screen in front of her. "You have two appointments already here," she said, staring at him with wide eyes.

He understood her meaning: Mr Maclean. He was an elderly man with a chihuahua, and he deemed himself late if he was ten minutes early. No doubt his appointment wasn't even for another half an hour, if not more.

Grinning, he nodded his head. "I'll get the room set up. Give me ten minutes."

"Sure thing."

He wandered down the hallways, hearing conversations in the rooms he passed, and opened the door to his domain. He dropped his backpack to the floor of his office and draped his coat on a hook on the back of the door. Threading his fingers through his hair, he ruffled it and yawned. He loved his choice of jobs, but sometimes, he thought he'd taken on too much. Honestly, though, he could slow down at the shelter because he was doing more than they paid for anyway, but he loved it too much to stop.

When he'd first broached the idea of decreasing his hours at the clinic and working at the shelter instead, Rory had tried to change his mind, thinking Heath would miss the clinic. After talking it through some more, Rory had seen what Heath was saying, and he'd approached Klaus about working there. Klaus had been happy about it and insisted on paying him for his time. Heath had tried to argue but had lost.

"Petal and Mrs Sanderson, would you like to come in," he called from the edge of the waiting room.

Watching the young woman weave her way through the chairs with the cat carrier, Heath smiled, knowing he had the best of both worlds.

· • • ● ● · ● ● • • ·

"I'm so glad you went for a takeaway. I feel like we've not had it for ages," Heath said in between mouthfuls.

Rory snorted. "You mean ages since we had Chinese last week?"

Heath paused. "Oh, yeah. I'd forgotten about that." He chuckled. "I'm getting old."

"No, you're not."

"It feels it some days." He put down his fork and wiped his mouth. "I had been thinking..."

"That's dangerous." Rory smirked. "What have you been thinking about?" He leaned his arms on the table, giving Heath his undivided attention, something that always warmed Heath's heart.

He fingered the edge of his plate while he stared at the table, his heart pounding. "Do you want kids?" he whispered.

There was silence for a moment before Rory's hand cupped Heath's chin, lifting his head. The smile on his face was beautiful. "I'd love to have some kids. Would you?"

Heath nodded as much as he could with Rory's hand holding him. "I—" His voice cracked, and he cleared his throat. "I would like some to go with our dogs."

"The quintessential family life would be amazing, Heath. We certainly have room for them now that they finished the extension." Heath let out a sigh, making Rory chuckle and release him. "Did you think I wouldn't?"

Heath waggled his head from side to side. "I wasn't sure, to be honest. I know you love Brody and Drew, but I also know how difficult your childhood was. I didn't know for certain whether you would be up for the idea because of how your parents were."

# 26

# Rory

Rory smiled when his words reminded him of how amazing Heath was. "Thank you, but it's because of them I know what not to do. I would love to have kids. Whenever we both agree to it."

"How about now?"

Rory raised his eyebrows. "Now?" He felt tingles running down his spine and tried not to show how he was feeling.

"Well, obviously, not right this second, but what about we look into it? I don't know which route would be best for us: adoption, surrogacy, foster care. Maybe we can look into the options first and see what needs to be done before we decide which one to do."

"Sounds good to me." He knew his smile was radiant, but he couldn't help it. "I would love to have a mini-you around the place."

"And I a mini-you."

Rory chuckled. "Well, I think we definitely need to check out surrogacy then. See what's involved."

Heath's face lit up, and he gripped Rory's hands. "Really?"

Rory nodded, grinning at Heath's obvious excitement. "Sure. It's bound to take a while before we decide, so why not start looking now?"

Heath stood, his chair scraping backwards, and threw his arms around Rory's neck. Rory rubbed a hand up and down Heath's back, soothing him.

"Thank you."

Rory pulled back. "You don't have to thank me."

"Yeah, I do. You're amazing, and I love you more every day."

"And I you, sweetheart." Rory took Heath's mouth in a soft caress.

Their lovemaking that evening was tender and sweet—after Rory had ravaged Heath on the kitchen table, that was.

• • • ● • ● ● • • ·

Rory blew out a breath and stretched out his neck a little, wincing when knots tugged at him. He'd have to sweet talk Heath into giving him a back massage when he got home.

"You really should let someone take that work off your hands, you know."

Rory's head shot up at his sister's voice. "What are you doing here?" He stood, rounding the desk and giving her a hug. "Where are the rugrats?"

"Huh, nice. No one cares about me. Only the kids I popped out."

Rory knew she was only messing with him. "Yep, no one cares about the mother."

Aggie chuckled. "They're with Heath's parents. I'm back for work."

"What? No, it's too early—"

"I've had my year of maternity leave, Rory. I'm fine. And it looks like you could do with some help, anyway." She pushed him aside and sank into his chair. "What did you do to the process I created before I left?"

Rory rolled his lips inwards. "Um, well..."

Aggie sighed. "Never mind. I'll fix it." She began moving pieces of paper, and Rory knew she had dismissed him.

He chuckled, walking down the corridors until he exited into the sunshine. Klaus had been good to them. As soon as he'd realised Aggie was there, he'd offered her an admin job—in other words, doing the paperwork that Rory hated. She'd said no originally because she hadn't wanted to leave them understaffed while she had Drew, but Klaus had persuaded her it was fine, and she would get all the maternity leave she otherwise wouldn't have received.

His generosity had overwhelmed Aggie and Rory, but he knew Klaus was a force to be reckoned with once he got an idea in his head. The same thing went for Carlton.

Speaking of, "Hey! I haven't seen you yet today. Why are you hiding from me?"

Carlton shook his head. "Because if I hear one more question about how I know Klaus, I'm going to deck you."

"Why not just tell me then? Then I won't ask anymore." Rory smirked.

Carlton sighed. "None of your business, mate." He reached for a bucket full of water and walked off.

Rory watched when Nolan waylaid him, stepping close and gesturing wildly with his hands. Carlton appeared to listen for a moment, then shook his head and weaved around the other man. Nolan grabbed his arm, stopping him, raising his hand to grip Carlton's shirt. They both hesitated before Carlton pulled away.

Rory raised his eyebrows and stared at the expression on Nolan's face while he watched Carlton walk away. After, Nolan glanced at the ground and headed to the shed.

Not understanding what he'd witnessed between the two men, he strode to the kennels, ready to take out the most rambunctious of them all for a run around the enclosed field. Klaus had paid for the entire field to be completely escape-proof so the dogs could have free rein—with a human supervisor, of course.

He loved his job, and he'd love it even more if he could help bring up children surrounded by animals.

Barking preceded him, and he laughed when the dogs jumped up at the fences surrounding their kennels.

"Yeah, hold on, hold on. I can't take you all at once."

* * * * * * * * * *

*Two years later*

Rory paced the corridor of the hospital in front of Heath, who was sitting, wringing his hands together. No one had been out to see them in ages, and he was getting worried. He knew childbirth took a long time sometimes, but he wanted everyone to be all right. He could never forgive himself if something happened to either the mother or the baby.

"Everything is fine, Rory," Heath's dad said, wrapping an arm around his shoulders. "Heath, they will be fine."

"But it's earlier than it was supposed to be. She still had another five weeks to go."

"And they are in the best place to make sure nothing happens. Early pregnancies happen all the time. Just be patient."

Rory sat next to Heath and laid his head on his shoulder, closing his eyes and trying to breathe through the panic.

"Rory? Heath? You can come through now."

His head shot up when his nurse's voice called for them. Both scrambled to their feet and raced down the corridor. Rory peeked into the hospital room and was waved in. He pulled Heath in behind him and drifted over to the bed. The woman who had given them the most precious gift of all lay tiredly with a beautiful smile.

"Thank you so much, Aggie. You can't understand how much we appreciate everything you have done for us." He leaned down and rested his forehead against his sister's.

When she had first offered to be their surrogate, they had been shocked. They hadn't expected her to want to do it when she had not long had her own kids. She had joked that this was the best time for her to do it—when she was still in the throes of not wanting another baby of her own. They'd finally agreed, and Heath had been the first. They had used donor eggs instead of Aggie's because it had seemed a bit too close for comfort for them, and besides, when Rory had his turn, he couldn't exactly use Aggie's eggs then. They'd certainly had a laugh over that when they'd thought about it. This way, their children would have the same 'mother' and each of them as a father.

"I know, Rory. Trust me, I know."

He lifted his tear-stained face and smiled with a trembling chin while he turned to where the bundle of joy laid in the small cot. Heath was already staring at the small baby wrapped tightly in a blanket.

"Hello, little one. Welcome to the world," he whispered, stroking a finger down the baby's cheek.

"You can pick her up, you know," Aggie joked from the bed.

Rory glanced at Heath and nodded for him to go first. He watched when Heath reached out and lifted their daughter, cradling her against his chest while he came closer. Rory wrapped his arm around Heath's waist and peered down at their daughter. She had a head full of straight, red hair, and her skin was wrinkly; no one had ever seemed more perfect.

As he stood there, enclosing Heath and their daughter, Elodie, in his arms, he finally felt like he was home.

$$\bullet \, \bullet \, \bullet \, \bullet \, \bullet \, \bullet \, \bullet \, \bullet \, \bullet \, \bullet$$

If you want to find out more about Heath's problems with Alex and the issues with Casey, you'll need to read the Crush series. Read on for a teaser of Instant Desire, which is the first book in the Crush series.

And you'll receive a free short story, exclusive content and updates if you sign up to my newsletter.

# Instant Desire Teaser

**Sean**

Sean checked his watch after he'd parked the car, noticing he was early, as usual. He hated being late, so he always ended up waiting around for the correct time before heading to his appointment. *Better early than late*, his father always said. But he sometimes wondered how much of his time was spent waiting around.

He pulled out the folder containing the information on his next client, and even though he had it memorised, he flicked through it again. Asher Danvers wanted a two-car garage conversion into a secured self-contained unit with access to the garden area. It seemed simple enough, but Sean would have to wait and see what Mr Danvers said in person. Sean had realised early on in this job that what information was passed on over the phone, was not always everything the client had on their mind.

Eyeing his watch again, he blew out a breath. He had another five minutes before he could go without appearing to be ridiculously early for the appointment. Max had always laughed about this quirk of his, but that was because Max was always late.

Sean had met Max Hughes, by chance, at a bar in Sean's sixth year of architecture and Max's first year of interior design. They were both attending different universities in Cambridge and had been trying to gain the bartender's attention. They'd ended up in conversation, then decided to join their respective parties together for a huge night out.

So, when Sean had accepted the offer at TAC, he had come armed with knowledge of an interior designer, who he had incorporated into some of his jobs as soon as Max had qualified. Max was grateful, and his business had boomed with the referrals he'd received from Sean. They were a good team.

Sean checked his watch once more and smiled, three minutes early exactly. He climbed out of the car, holding tight to the folder as he shut the door and headed to Mr Danvers' front door. He could see the two garages that Mr Danvers wanted converted, and they looked in reasonable condition, but Sean would withhold judgement until he saw the inside—that was where many properties let their owners down.

Walking past the neatly kept garden to the front door, Sean knocked. He gazed around as he waited for an answer, which when it came, heralded a figure he had not expected.

Mr Danvers was no older man wanting to make a live-in unit for his family to visit, which is what Sean had envisaged. No, Mr Danvers was a gorgeous, six-foot, brown-haired, golden-eyed wonder with scruff that looked like it would feel amazing on Sean's skin.

Sean was startled from his musings with that thought and quickly held out his hand. "Mr Danvers? I'm Sean Edwards from Thompson Architect Company." He cleared his throat as he waited for the guy to welcome him.

"Ah, yes, hello." He shook Sean's hand. "Please, call me Asher."

They stood facing each other for a moment before a loud crash, silence, then a screaming cry sounded from within. Sean jumped as Asher spun around and raced down the hallway Sean could see from the front door.

Sean wasn't quite sure what to do. He'd not been invited in, but he didn't want to stand here and leave the door open. He decided to step inside and shut the door behind him. Waiting in the large entryway, Sean studied his surroundings briefly—stairs to the right side and dark wood flooring as far as the eye could see. He could see the open plan living room through an archway to the left and a similarly presented dining room to the right. Straight ahead, he saw another door.

He heard talking from further inside, so he decided to follow the sound, making sure his footsteps were heard as he approached what he thought was the kitchen.

Entering the kitchen, his assumption being correct, he saw that Asher was on his knees cradling a child in his arms as he talked in soft tones. Asher peered up at him, and Sean saw panic in his eyes.

"Could you get me some ice, please?" Sean saw Asher indicate the freezer on the other side of the kitchen. He paused, then went over to do as asked. Finding an ice pack, he looked around for a towel and wrapped it up before handing it to Asher.

"Is he all right?" Sean asked.

Grab the book here : https://books2read.com/instantdesire

# Books by Elouise East

**Illuminate Matchmaking**
Ignite
Blaze
Kindle
Scorch

**Club Royal**
Royal Firsts
Rogue Royal
Secretive Royal
Grieving Royal
Disowned Royal
Trained Royal
Awakened Royal
Commanding Royal

**Boys, Daddies, Snuggles & More**
Need Him
Trust Him

**Daddy**
Love Me, Daddy
Soothe Me, Daddy

A SPECIAL LOVE

Spoil Me, Daddy
The Complete Daddy Series

**Love in Flames**
Out of the Frying Pan
Smokescreen
Breathing Fire
Love in Flames Collection

**Crush**
Love Conquers
Instant Desire
Primary Seduction
Deep Down
A Crush for Christmas
Life Support
Covert Strength
Love Scene
Lawful Attraction
Crush Collection Volume 1
Crush Collection Volume 2
Crush Collection Volume 3

**Just A Little Crush**
First Kiss
He's Behind You
A Special Love
Three Thirds
Sweet Truths

**Standalone**
Treehouse Whispers
Star-Crossed

Protecting the Thief
Sizzling Chauffeur

**<u>Elouise R East (taboo)</u>**
**Dark & Divergent**
Forbidden Temptation
Too Many Secrets

**Collide**
When Fantasies Collide
When Dreams Collide
When Pleasures Collide
When Cravings Collide

# About the Author

Elouise East writes sweet and steamy connections in gay romance. She also touches on taboo stories under the name Elouise R East.

Books that tell the stories where friendship and family are the focal point - be it blood family or chosen - are very important to her. That's why she includes a variety of personalities, talents, ages, situations and abilities as she believes a story or character needs. She wants her characters to be real, to be relatable, to be free to have whatever views they tell her they have. And trust her, most of the time, she does not have *any* say in the matter!

Her characters come to life on the page for her as well as her readers. Their stories unfold in front of her as she writes, and she has very little input into how they want to be shown. Just like real life, the lives of her characters change with every choice, every interaction and every conversation. And she wouldn't have it any other way.

She writes books that are emotionally realistic, even if liberties are taken with other aspects of the stories. She doesn't know any other way to write. It comes from deep inside.

Who is she? A single parent to two children living in the UK. An avid reader who still tries to devour every book she can get her hands on. A student of learning about any subject that takes her fancy. An author of books she would read herself. And a romantic at heart who loves anything cheesy.

Who's joining her on her journey?